THE
CHAOS
FACTOR

BILL WATSON

authorHOUSE®

AuthorHouse™ UK
1663 Liberty Drive
Bloomington, IN 47403 USA
www.authorhouse.co.uk
Phone: UK TFN: 0800 0148641 (Toll Free inside the UK)
UK Local: 02036 956322 (+44 20 3695 6322 from outside the UK)

Published by AuthorHouse 08/19/2021

ISBN: 978-1-6655-9238-3 (sc)
ISBN: 978-1-6655-9240-6 (hc)
ISBN: 978-1-6655-9239-0 (e)

Print information available on the last page.

This book is printed on acid-free paper.

PROLOGUE

M IDNIGHT. THE RAF JUNIOR TECH, SITTING SLUMPED, COLLAR undone, tie off, chained by his ears to a pair of powerful Racal radio receivers, stirred uneasily. It was silly, but he felt he had a personal ghost. Sitting in a row with sixty linguists and other W.Op.Specs—special radio operators—in a brightly lit, fluorescent, antiseptic mega-Tardis of a room, he felt haunted.

He sat up, alert. Here it came again. The Morse: faint, wavering, ghostly, rising and falling on waves of static. It spooked him. Every month it came on mids—his night-watch—just on midnight, faint, weird, but inexorable. Beating out five-letter groups ... SDCPK ... ABDIX ... HFNMO ... TPROV ... lasting just thirty seconds. That was not in itself surprising; there was always static and other stations, commercial and military, drifting in and out of his frequency. But there were two things about it that worried him.

Firstly (and he hardly dared admit it to himself), every day following the transmission, there was a major crime, a disaster, or an act of terrorism. A pit-disaster. An aeroplane exploding on take-off. Once an armed bank raid. A major pile-up on one of the new motorways. Violent anti-Vietnam riots.

Coincidence? He sincerely hoped so ... but ... for the five years he had been on this camp, that wavering, lunatic Morse had presaged a disaster every month. Or had it?

The other thing bothering him was that he couldn't read the sender. He was a capable and experienced special operator. He could recognise a sender by the "fist"—the way the individual operated the Morse-key. He usually had a Russian civvy air net and had his own regulars who he recognised when their shifts crossed his. He even gave them nicknames:

Ivan, Grigor, Fyodor, and Natasha. He thought that fist sounded delicate and female. And even when they got bored or secretive and changed to the other hand, he could recognise them.

Yet this ghost of his … no way could he get a toehold on it. It was always the same hand, but sent in a wavering, illogical way that defied description.

At the ripe old age of 25, he thought he knew everything there was to know about Morse, but this one had him beat. It wasn't Russian, East German, Polish, Czech, or even Chinese. Neither was it a side-to-side bug-key. This bugged him so much he had asked his watch commander if he could listen to the old training tapes, and the only thing he could liken it to was an old tape of a wartime Lancaster bomber. Despite the bright normality of the section, he shivered.

And it was too fast to be a radio ham, he uneasily reminded himself.

The camp, a fighter station in the war, was full of ghost stories—headless navigators and strange lights—but there could *not* be a ghost Lancaster limping home out there. How in 1968 could a Lancaster be out there sending five-letter groups? And no one official used old-fashioned imprecise valve-set radios anymore. In fact, very few people alive even knew how to use such technology. When in '67 they refurbished an old Lancaster, they had to dig out a retired flight lieutenant to teach someone how to drive it. Yet someone was using '40s technology to send what, by their very format, had to be military or security messages in 1968.

It needn't mean anything—could be a kid playing with an old set or a radio ham having to use obsolete equipment. It had to be a coincidence. Or had five years chained to two Racals sent him doolalley? Yet it worried him. Kids send gobbledygook, and hams are slow and don't use five-letter groups; those are strictly military.

He made his mind up. He might look like a superstitious fool, and he'd probably be laughed at or sent to the sickbay, but so what? It bugged him. He needed answers.

He automatically sat up straighter and fastened his collar and the sta-bright buttons on his uniform jacket. He reached for the intercom. "Sir …" he said.

The next day, the East Coast express derailed after hitting two black painted concrete-filled barrels just outside Peterborough. The driver and seven passengers died instantly, leaving twenty more in hospital.

1

I T WAS 6.30 A.M. THE BIG RED ALARM WITH THE TWO HUGE BELLS WENT off. Its strident clamour slashed through the man's subconscious. He groaned, hit the alarm button, and rolled out of bed.

The early-morning light reluctantly shed its meagre blessing upon the room as he pulled back the curtain. He went over to the cold tap in the corner of his one-room shack and splashed his face and body; gasped and grinned; and then rubbed himself down with the coarse white towel from the back of the plank door. He breathed deeply in and out three times and, naked and goosefleshed, went to the ex-WD steel wardrobe for a grey tracksuit, T-shirt, M&S underpants, woolly socks, and running shoes. He pulled them on, lithe and hard-fleshed, and tied the shoes with an almost old-lady finickiness.

He opened the door and stood outside, waving arms and legs in the esoteric patterns of tai chi. Then, with the conscious effort of a swimmer diving into cold water, he plunged into the morning chill. He jogged steadily down the cliff path and onto the sand. As he ran, the beach stretched away seemingly to infinity in front of him.

His mood changed. Endorphins kicked in. Joy lifted his steps, lightened his heart, and brought a smile to his hatchet features. His steps quickened. His head went back.

It began to rain, big drops splashing on the sand ahead of him, dappling his T-shirt, exhilarating him. His smile turned into a great boyish grin. He leapt. He cavorted. He turned cartwheels. "Hallelujah!" he shouted. "Hallelujah!"

It was 6.30 a.m. The alarm dragged me into a sort of consciousness. I groaned. The almost-blonde head beside me groaned too. Nessie, Vanessa, my latest bit of capurtle, levered herself out of bed and put the kettle on. Life-saving coffee.

After the third cup of coffee and two Alka-Seltzers, as consciousness pulsed through my veins and the little men with hammers toned it down a bit, my stomach progressively leadened and my sluggish spirits lowered even further. I reluctantly dragged on the bog-trotting cords, the T-shirt and socks, and tied the desert wellies' laces with fingers like unhelpful sausages.

Many times I have obeyed orders I didn't want to, but I *really* didn't want to go to Yorkshire. It wasn't the late night; coming out of a folk club at 2.30 a.m. was only average for me. It wasn't the *vin plonque* that was lapping its sludge around my stomach or the little men with hammers. Hangovers I can deal with. It wasn't even the reluctance to leave a warm pliable blonde and a warm pliable bed. It was the idea of crawling across London to King's Cross station and being expensively whisked by one of BR's Deltic diesels up to York, getting a hire car, and driving to the North Yorkshire coast to recruit my former watch commander.

This idea of making such a wasted journey irritated me immensely. He was wanted for a top-secret, your-eyes-only job. And I knew he'd refuse. And to follow this wild goose, I had been pulled off an investigation into home-grown terrorism that was ready to go.

Now this ex-boss of mine—and, if I'm honest, a good mate—was a card-carrying lunatic. A genuine head-the-ball. I suppose if your name's John Gallipoli Smith, you're bound to be a bit eccentric. But this guy had raised eccentricity to an art form. I don't mean he had unusual deviancies or fancied sheep; he had been happily married. He was quiet, reasonable, and low-key, but he could make logic stand on its head and argue his way out of the gates of hell.

He had a massive IQ; was fluent in Russian, French, German, and Polish; was master of arts in political science and a seventh-dan judo; and was just the best cryptographer in the business. But mad as a whole factory of hatters.

He'd always been eccentric, but after his wife and daughter had died two years earlier—foggy day, greasy road, skidding tanker—he'd really gone off the rails. He was always a bit of a churchgoer, but after losing his family, he got religion even worse, resigned from the job, sold up, and now lived in a shack above Whitby. He lived a simple life (and for *simple* read "plain crazy"), praying, reading, and navel-gazing. And I figured that by now, his navel was probably talking back to him.

He and I had worked together a lot—first as beat bobbies, then in one of the more esoteric branches of the Met, vaguely Special Branch but reporting straight to the Home Office. We were an odd little antiterrorist organisation, and so far under the radar as to be almost subterranean. Trained by the Marine SBS, we worked as commandos—heavy backup for busting organised crime and as stiffening for local SPGs and antiterrorist units just as the IRA began to show their faces again. Not forgetting that Baader–Meinhof was being silly, and of course, the Russian Bear was very much using his claws.

We had to be skilled in all sorts of naughtiness and counter-naughtiness, from psychology to picking locks, weaponry, cryptography, explosives, and unarmed combat. We had normally skulked in an attic in one of those big terraced houses near Euston Station, disguised as a university political analysis department.

But times had moved on, and I was currently flying an antiterrorist desk in Whitehall. Smithy was incommunicado in Whitby. And I was supposed to go and enlist his radio-intercept and cryptography skills because some RAF berk had logged a funny that was just funny enough to get our Beloved Masters in Whitehall spooked. An unclassified transmission had wandered onto a Russian civilian air-traffic net—and it wasn't Radio Caroline. It was an obsolete burst of Morse, after which there always seemed to follow an accident, a disaster, a bit of chaos. And I had been instructed to recruit John, find out if the chaos was coincidence, and if not, track the transmitter, break the code, and arrest whomever.

In this day of massive espionage by all sides in the Cold War—and Philby & Co, Profumo, and Vassall still playing at their bowler-hatted inner-mind cinemas—our masters were passing bricks that they might be missing something. *Who needs a ghost in their personnel files?* I grumpily meditated. And when I had demanded answers—as GCHQ, Five, and Six were crawling with cryptographers—I was told, "Shut up and do as you're told. Smith is deniable." I was not reassured.

But as I got off the train at York, then picked up the hired Cortina 1600E and drove it across the North York moors, gradually the height, the openness, and the blustery wind rocking the car brought a gleam of sunshine into my soul. The little men with hammers went off for lunch, the volcano in my stomach relapsed into a grumble, and the gloom receded. So what if they had sent me instead of a telegram? It was a day out, and their capitation.

I found myself mulling over this funny my masters had found. At first, tempted to lose the communication and file it under wpb, they remembered Philby, Burgess and McLean, Profumo, and Vassall, and how with such a mighty glop they had all hit the fan. Someone panicked; someone fairly high in the pecking order started an inquiry and went off to change his trousers. So the Beloved Führers had fed a query into the GCHQ mainframe, and its cold electronic heart had spat out Smithy's name. So Muggins here, low down the pecking order, had to go and try to recruit him. I categorically didn't want to be doing this; he couldn't be bribed, he couldn't be blackmailed, he couldn't be cajoled, and after all, he did have a right to his own life. So here was I, going to try to build bricks without straw. I racked my brain to work out a way of approaching Smithy and finally gave up.

But what would our striped-trousered Whitehall Warriors think if I failed? I swallowed my pride and resentment and thought of my pension. After all, Smithy was only human ... I think. And if the Whitehall Wonders wanted to send me two hundred miles on expenses in a pretty posh car chasing wild geese, instead of sending a telegram, who was I to cocoa? Who says the Home Office doesn't waste money? He might not even be there.

Then I thought of Nessie left in my bed, and lust and regret flowed through my psyche. I gave the branny Cortina 1600E its head along the A64. Hmm! Pretty nippy, and clinging to the road like an Aberdonian to a sixpence. Soaring past the sci-fi mushrooms of Fylingdales, giant extraterrestrial fungi ready to give us a whole four minutes warning of doom, I pulled into Whitby, booked into a cheap but clean boarding house, and set off to find Smithy.

I drove through the fish-stinking harbour three miles along the cliff road and drew up at a forlorn little shed—a transplanted beach hut, thunderbox bog at the back. Smithy's des res.

4

Quick knock on the door, and there stood Smithy, eyes and mouth rounded in surprise, gobsmacked but genial. He had always been on the skinny side, whipcord rather than Mr Universe, but he seemed even thinner, face gaunt to the point of emaciation, mouth enclosed in parentheses, but seemingly bright-eyed and bushy-tailed. His face split into an amazed watermelon grin.

"Bill, you old ratbag, what brings you up here? Fleshpots of the Smoke getting too much?" I was dragged inside and seated in a lumpy excuse for an armchair whilst Smithy went to put the kettle on. "Good to see you, mate! What's dragged you up here? I thought you never left the Smoke these days," Smithy rabbited on.

I took a surreptitious look around. The walls were covered floor to ceiling with books, higgledy-piggledy, theology next to Agatha Christie and philosophy next to Len Deighton. Then a battered ex-WD wardrobe, khaki green; ex-WD iron cot, blankets folded square, hospital-cornered; two superannuated chairs; and a kettle, portable cooker, and sink. Nothing else.

"You doing OK, Smithy?" I asked, pity flooding me. "You ever hanker about a bit more luxury?" I remembered Smithy, for all his religion and teetotalism, being the life and soul of many a party. I remembered him, arm round his wife, Alicia, as he gazed fondly at 2-year-old Bethany's tricks. And to come to this.

"No, this is enough for me, Bill," Smithy spoke over his shoulder. "When Alicia and Bethany died, I just needed to get out. I needed a life of my own and a grief of my own. So I got out, claimed my superann, and sought solitude. Now I feel at home here. Look at that view. Listen to the silence. I needed that, and now it's grown on me."

Smithy put down two steaming mugs, Donald Duck and A Present From Morecombe, full of gungy-looking coffee, moving a big black book to do so. I peered at the title. A Bible.

"But what do you find to do all day?" I was genuinely interested. "How come you're not so bored you're talking to the furniture? Don't you miss the excitement? Remember when you saved my life chucking that murderous middle-clarse pseud and his silly home-made bomb through the window? I had to change trousers after that!" I smiled wryly and added, "Too much Red Brigade, too much sixth-form politics, too much time, too many rich daddies, and not enough sense."

Smithy grinned. "Yes, it was a bit exciting, that! I thought we were both goners. I lost a gallon of adrenaline that day!"

We talked over old times as the Old and Bold always do. We'd been through a lot together, me and Smithy, on the sharp end of a very chilly cold war.

"I suppose I do miss the excitement," he admitted. "This was a real culture change, but I do a lot of talking." Smithy grinned wryly. "But not to the furniture—I pray and meditate. Every day, I jog and do tai chi and judo. I read and I swim a lot, sea or local pool. And if I feel the need for company, I nip down to a caff or the library in Whitby and chat. I go to church. I have friends." He paused reflectively. "I understand how the old hermits found peace."

"Oh! In that case, I don't reckon you'll like my next question," I began, trailing my coat.

Smithy's ears pricked up. "And what would that be, you conniving ratbag? Tell me why this social call."

"Whitehall has got its knickers in a twist about an unofficial transmission that keeps straying onto and jamming a Russian civilian Morse net that's also used by their air force, and nastiness seems to follow." I scratched my chin. "We don't even know if this is real; could easily be something and nothing. But you know how tetchy our Sleepless Guardians are at the minute. And so they've come up with me and you to sort it."

Smithy frowned. "Why me? I've been out of the racket two years now. It's all behind me, and I have no hankering to come back."

I grinned cynically. "Because you're good at this stuff. Because this is all under the table. Because they want deniability. Because you and I are cheaper and less official than putting all the sneaky-beakies of Five, Special Branch, and Q on it. and we can be blamed if it goes wrong. Backsides covered with exquisite tailoring. It's called hedging their bets."

Smithy considered. "I'll need to ask the Boss. Give me tonight to pray and think. Now, can I offer you some fried rice and vegetables?"

I tried not to shudder. "No thanks. I'm booked in down the road. I'll be back at eight tomorrow."

And after being enveloped in a sweaty man hug, I went my way.

2

I HAD A CONVIVIAL NIGHT NATTERING TO LOCAL FISHERMEN AND fishers of tourists in the hotel bar. I had no more than two pints of Guinness and flirted—but no more—with a large and voluptuous lady: white kinky boots, red wet-look jacket, and short skirt, indeterminate years but undoubted potential. But then her husband had taken her home, so I retired to bed at a reasonable hour.

Hence I was up and at Smithy's place at 7.45, breakfasted and dressed in my best official guise: smart Italian suit, pink shirt, and Guards-like tie.

He was already up, toast in hand, dressed, and looking quite smart for him: old but good grey suit, check shirt, tie, wingtip shoes, unruly blond hair combed into submission.

"Where to?" he asked.

"RAF Mugglesby, in Lincolnshire," I responded.

"I know it well," he grunted. "The Sahara with grass, where they monitor all sorts of radio broadcasts, ours and theirs. I did a spell there years ago as a Russian linguist."

"Yes, it was a junior technician W.Op.Spec down there that first put us on to that funny."

"So we'll need equipment. What are they giving us?"

I shrugged. "What we want, as we want, when we want it. But keep the expense down."

"My totally hypothetical goodness, our Beloved Führers really must be wetting their drawers. Either that, or using up their annual allocation before the end of the year." He added a quizzical glance.

"Too early, still six months to go," I replied cynically. "I reckon they must at least suspect something naughty is going down. Remember, *Christine and the Defence Secretary* is still playing at their personal cinemas, not to mention Vassall, Kim Philby, and various other naughtinesses in Moscow. They are worried! Otherwise, why throw all the equipment we ask for and a bit of £.s.d. at us? I reckon this could be for real; it could just be much more than an exercise for press or Parliament."

"You could be right, but if you're not, they are in the clear."

"Precisely."

The journey down was mostly silent. I insisted on driving. Smithy, for all his delicacy of movement and bodily awareness, was a lousy driver. So he sat in the passenger seat and read his Bible. I honestly didn't think my driving was that bad.

By mid-morning, we were driving through the single red-and-white horizontal pole that guarded the camp entrance—real IRA-stopper, that one pole—along with one Snowdrop, an RAF copper. After a bit of low-IQ hampering and working to rule by the duty corporal, and a bit of rank-pulling, warrant-card waving and insisting on "sir" by us, we managed to get into station headquarters, past the station warrant officer, and in to the CO, who, surprisingly, had been expecting us.

At this point, Smithy took over. "Now, Wing Commander, I want to see the J/T who logged this. I also want to see the files of those logs, and in particular, I want to see any direction-finding info you may have."

Not a bad bit of rank-pulling from a guy who left the air force as a mere corporal.

The J/T in question was presented to the CO's office within half an hour, Best Blue in evidence, cap under arm.

"547 J/T McIntosh, Sir!"

"First name, laddie?" Smithy grunted.

"Paul, sir." He was standing strictly to attention, uniform hastily donned, ready for a rollocking. A call to SHQ is never comfortable.

"Right, Paul. Let's cut out the formal rubbish. You're not on a charge. I'm John Smith, unemployed and unattached civilian, and this Neanderthal man is Bill Watson, who's a superintendent in the fuzz, sort of. If we are to work together, it's on my terms, which are first-name: I'm John, this is Bill. So, Wing Commander, would you organise some coffee for us while we wait for the Section to remember which cup the reports are filed under?"

We sat down, Smithy and I at ease, Paul cringing with embarrassment, whilst the CO dispensed coffee, pop-eyed and bristly moustached, with lese-majesty and disapproval.

"Nice tight ship you run here, CO," Smithy said, pouring oil on troubled Wingcos. Verbal judo had always been Smithy's speciality—keep 'em off balance.

"Now, Paul," he said, turning to the J/T. "What made you get on to Matey?"

"Well, sir …"

"John!"

"Well, er … *John*, I've been on the same watch ever since I was posted here, five years ago, and sitting on the same frequency. It's a Russian civilian Voice/Morse net, Aeroflot International, Kiev Control. But the VVS also use it." Warming up as enthusiasm took over from nerves, he continued, "And once a month, this joker comes up on Morse. It's not as far away as Russia, and it's very wavery; old, obsolete valve technology. It's fairly quick; experienced fist, but no trouble following it, get 100 per cent of take every time. But it's very short—thirty seconds max." Paul paused and frowned. "It was so regular across my frequ, I started logging it for fun and to ease the boredom. Then I happened to notice that one or two days after, the *Mirror* would report a disaster somewhere in mainland UK. Bombings, shootings, major crashes. So I got onto the watch commander, and we logged it properly and D/F-ed it. The direction finders didn't come up with much; too short a time. Just a fix—vaguely north-west England. But it's obviously important, cos you two are here."

"And you got no further?"

"Well, Christ!"

"Paul," Smithy interrupted, coldly, "I said you work on *my* terms. No blasphemy! Ever! Continue."

One very discomfited J/T resentfully asked, "Is it OK if I say 'bugger me'?" J/Ts are experts at pushing boundaries.

The ice in Smithy's eyes twinkled. He grinned. "It's OK if it's an exclamation and not an invitation."

Then, serious again, Paul said, "Well, sir—er, John—we did our best, but it's not really our scene. I even chased it up on training tapes. It just isn't long enough. So we sent the lot down to GCHQ with all the regular take."

"OK, Paul, I wasn't criticising, but I do need to know everything—absolutely everything, even the unscientific gut reactions. Bill and I are going to have to turn you inside out for the next three weeks. Then maybe we'll be ready for Himself; armed and ready to go."

Just then, a general duties corporal shoved his short-back-and-sides round the door and told us the Section was ready for us.

The CO put us in his staff car, an aged but immaculate black Humber Hawk, and personally escorted us up to the Section. Whitehall must have been busy.

It was weird up there—the great poles of the aerial farm, the double doors like airlocks, barred like a jail, the little identity tags, then step forward into the twenty-third century, bright, clean, efficient, and soulless. The harsh glare of the fluorescents. The impersonal electronic faces of the double-banked Racal radio-receivers. And the operators, chained by the ears, zombies staring at nothing but occasionally coming to life and scribbling fitfully.

Then we were squeezed into a side room with the flight-lieutenant watch commander and the watch warrant officer.

"Right, gentlemen! Bill and I will be in your hair and up your noses a great deal. Bill?" Smithy handed over.

"We'll need to pick your brains," I continued, "and we'll need to be in here with the files a lot. So we need permanent ID tags, and can we have twenty-four-hour unrestricted access to this room? Can we also have entry restricted to us and a lock on the door?"

"Sir!" rang out from the warrant officer, grudgingly, understandably a bit suspicious. Sneaky-beakies always mean trouble.

"What will you need, Bill?" asked the CO.

"We'll need three detector vans—I'll arrange them with the Home Office—but we'll need to be patched into them from here. We'll need three crack operators, competent in D/F, one of whom to be J/T McIntosh, also to be given unrestricted entry into here."

"Right, sir," the watch commander barked. "I'll get three sergeants onto it right away."

"No you won't, Flight Lieutenant!" John interrupted. "I used to be in this racket too, and I remember what use sergeants were as operators! We'll have three corporals or J/Ts, please. We'll need your best, regardless of watch, but not highest-ranking. Sergeants tend to be rusty in operating. Too much time in the back room.

"Oh, right, sir. Anything else?"

"Yes. You'll have me on D/F at 00.00 Zulu on the night, and Superintendent Watson as overall supervisor." Smithy paused. "We'll need copies of everything you have on files, including any relevant signals to and from GCHQ, MOD, and the Home Office, and a corporal to handle the files and to patch us into GCHQ's mainframe."

"That should be easy for us, a working intercept unit."

"Right. Thank you, Flight Lieutenant. Now let's get down to serious business."

The next three weeks were, for me, a nice rest. Rather than attract too much attention round the camp, we stayed at a pub in Slagford: shared room, twin beds, a bit uncomfortable.

Slagford, the cemetery with lights. Rush hour is six tractors, the highlight of the week is the council cutting the grass, and the live entertainment is watching your knickers go round at the laundrette. But Thursday nights, there was a bit of a folk club in a pub run by a bunch of linguists and W.Op.Specs from the camp. I remember chortling at one of the lads, an Ulsterman, bog-trotting cords and Clancy Brothers sweater, three seas over, trying to sing "The Old Orange Flute" while slopping his pint.

Still, hanging round the Officers' Mess on the camp, I did manage to get off a couple of times with a pneumatic, Roedean-type flight lieutenant's wife while he was away in Germany. I'd get back to the hotel around midnight to find Smithy everlastingly on his knees. Poor sod. I'd had a few, so I asked, "Eh, Smithy lad, what do you find to pray about?" I sang softly:

And the next thing we'll pray for, we'll pray for a wench.
Glory O glory, please give us a wench.
And if we have one wench we might as well have ten.
Have a whole xxxing harem, said the Matelot. Amen!

Smithy was cold. "Don't presume, and don't clump into what you don't understand, Bill! Go and sleep it off."

Oops! Me and my big feet.

Thus the three weeks passed, and at five to midnight on the appointed night, we were crowded into our little cubbyhole: me, Smithy, the watch commander, the warrant officer i/c, the corporal clerk, the CO, and two operators—along with two radios, two tape recorders and a D/F set, all churning out heat. What with the air-conditioning not stretching to this room, the door locked, and the tension racking up, it was a bit reasty in there, to put it mildly. If we could have bottled the atmosphere, we could have used it for gassing vermin.

The two with headphones sat like slightly twitchy graven images, immobile, hands on tape buttons, eyes fixed on signal meters. The spare operator sat, pseudo-blasé, tie loose, jacket undone, whilst Paul, whose baby it was, exhibited tension twitches all down his body. Us non-combatants shuffled our feet, checked our watches, whispered about *any time now*, and all tried to fit round the map table.

Midnight, 00.00 Zulu, came and went. Tension bit like an adder, and just when we thought we'd blown it, along came the Morse. Faint, unreal, wavery, but there: SDCPK ... ABCXF ... DFYTU ... BEXNO ... AKLUI ... DFYT ... Then, after fifteen seconds, it was completely swamped by a gormless great Russian voice, "Vas ponyal, syemsot sorok tree, na svyaz." *(Understood, seven four three. On air.)*

I groaned with frustration, but Smithy was hopping with excitement.

"Got 'im! Got the ratbag! Get the map, Paul! Bill, get on to the other D/F stations!" He chortled. I've never seen anyone chortle before, but he did. He actually chortled.

He spread his gangly body out over the large-scale, extremely detailed map and, as the other D/F cross-references came in, drew the directional lines.

We had known it was vaguely north-west, so we had put a van in Carlisle, one in Prestatyn, and one in Leeds. And the cross-references put Charlie somewhere near Southport, on the north-west coast. But unfortunately, the signal was so wavery and of such short duration that even Superstar Smithy couldn't put it more accurately than that.

"OK, lads, now we wait for tomorrow's headlines. Till then, we can all relax."

Smithy and I, all euphoria gone, drove back to Sleaford and bed.

We heard on the news the next day that a Britannia Airways trooping flight for Berlin from Luton had run out of runway, aborted take-off, and crashed, killing pilot, first officer, and seven passengers, and injuring thirty more passengers, three seriously. Too much of a coincidence.

"More chaos," I told Smithy, "just like Paul suspected. More meaningless mayhem, more wreckage for wreckage's sake. That was a bog-standard trooping flight, no one special on it, just ordinary pongos. And supposed to achieve what?"

I saw from the sick look on Smithy's face and the clouding in his eyes that this had now got through to him.

"Oh," he said. "Oh, not very kind at all, a bit naughty, this." Very quiet, very low-key, very far away. I suddenly felt very sorry for the guys behind this.

No one else on the team noticed anything, but now it was for real. Before this, Smithy was going along with it—because he was curious, because he reckoned his God had rubber-stamped it, or maybe just as a change from Whitby. But now he was committed. Some sense of moral outrage was prickled. Some anger had arisen. This was personal.

And that meant an uncomfortable ride for me. I mean, it's just another job, why be so hot and strong? It happens all the time. One grubby little clandestine battle follows another. But I knew I was about to get dragged along behind the juggernaut of Smithy's moral outrage.

3

B UT THE NEXT MONTH WAS ANTICLIMACTIC—JUST A SLOG. I MANAGED to get down from woolly-back country to the fleshpots a couple of weekends to see Nessie, but for the most, it was the daily round, the common task, which certainly didn't furnish all that I asked.

Regularly at 6 a.m., I would be awakened by Smithy creeping round as delicate as a rhino with corns. He would put on his tatty old grey tracksuit, jog round Sleaford, come back to sing hideously in the shower—sometimes torturing hymns, sometimes horribly murdering Beatles songs—then spend an hour on his knees. Then, after, a leisurely breakfast, it was the six-mile drive to Mugglesby, to be locked in our little room, like troglodytes, never to emerge till five o'clock.

Paul was chuffed to beans to get off shift and be seconded to us. We would dine on curled-up sandwiches and drink copious gallons of tea and coffee; pore over maps; discuss if, what, and maybe; fiddle with figures; drink more endless muddy coffee till we were flying; and get ready for next time. We discussed the groups till our heads ached, whether the groups were geographical, type of target, or if not, what?

Eventually, I stretched. "OK, guys, here are some conclusions," I said. "Firstly, the five-letter groups, as we suspected, are military-style, based on geography: the first one a receiver code, the next two probably large grid references, the last one a finer reference, possibly based on ordnance survey maps or local A-Zs. The last two letters may well be some sort of recognition code. So possibly, the way it works could be, for instance, if we were to blow up Mugglesby (an idea that you J/Ts would heartily endorse, I reckon!), the place would be pinpointed by the first four letters and the last would be *military installation, RAF camp*, or similar. But I have to tell you, this is still very much guesswork."

"But why would there need to be so many groups?" Paul asked. "It's totally different to the way Russian groups work on my net."

"Well, for example, this place is a large and complex area. So, obviously, you couldn't pinpoint one building or installation with just one group, much less one particular aircraft, as happened last month. Maybe more instructions: personnel tasked and kit needed. So we end up with a sort of Chinese box—references within references. And don't forget this is some twenty-odd years out of date."

"I still don't totally get the validity of all the groups," Paul admitted.

"I'm not sure," I mused. "It could be a dummy, or maybe a bit more info. For instance, this place could be described as a military installation, RAF camp, radio station, high-security unit, or as the locals all call this top-secret highly secure installation, 'that there spy place down the road'. That way we'd know exactly what to blow up. Or maybe it's a protocol of progressively finer tuning: first place, for instance, an RAF camp; second group, say, mess hall; third, a time for the target; fourth, an amount of charge; fifth, a go-code. But as the transmission time always seems to be 00.00 Zulu or a few seconds after, the whole thing may be a mixture of recognition codes, go-codes, security codes, and dummies. At this stage, we can't know. A codebook would be very useful. But, Paul lad, we should be able to approximate the geography so that next time, we'll be a bit readier!"

For the next two weeks, we slogged away at the chimp-work, trying to work out Chummy's grid references and listening to the whispers and gossip and *what the heck is it?* coming from the main set-room. Gut-crushing, eyeball-aching chimp-work, until we were just about giving up the will to live. Fed up with barely edible sandwiches, we would send Paul into Slagford for pasties, pies, and doughnuts. We also liberated a coffee machine from SHQ.

As the day got closer, we managed to get the other operators off shift as well to work with us. This was not always welcomed by the powers-that-be; this was an important SIGINT monitoring site, involved with serious Cold War intelligence, and we were a little scruffy iffy bunch of secret squirrels—and me and Smithy not even Air Force.

Neither were our efforts helped by the constipated minds and jealousy of some watch commanders and warrant officers, who resented us pinching their best operators, doing our clandestine goodness-knows-what in *their* section, and even being here at all. Our task wasn't always expedited by the work-to-the-rule-book attitude of some senior NCOs. Who was it said that "Air Force intelligence" was an oxymoron? And we certainly got our share of the morons. We went off at 5.30 weeknights with aching backs, red eyes, and buzzing ears.

Another difficulty was that most of the tapes logging our funny had been routinely wiped and reused. Thus our intel was very limited—only the last month or two. Put in the fact that rarely do newspapers report only one disaster a day, and you can see we were needle-hunting in a ginormous great haystack. And not even a magnet between us.

But eventually, we managed a tenable idea of how Matey worked. He seemed to like explosions; more of them than anything else, and limited to public, easy-access places. And, gradually, like a photograph in developer, a pattern began to emerge, and we got a possible grid-reference out of it.

Smithy untangled himself from his mainframe-access console, stretched, knocked a cup of cold coffee into the back of a tape recorder, and said, "Got it! I know what Matey's up to. Not really that clever. Repeats himself. And old hat! Very World War Two. That's what's confused us. Look!"

And when we looked closely, sure, it was simple. The groups came, as we saw, in five groups of five letters, repeated. As we suspected, the first was a "this-is-me" code. The next three were locations, in an ever-smaller series of grid references. The fourth group was a description: for instance, BEXNO was used before every air crash, ABIOK before every explosion, plus a few others we couldn't match. And the fifth group, when we managed to get it, which wasn't that often, seemed to be a fine description and a go-code. The later ones we couldn't crack.

We got the corporal office manager to draw the J/Ts' input onto the grid of a table-size large-scale map, and we put in each disaster and tried to cross-reference it with Matey's groups. We verified that the signals came from the South West Lancashire area and narrowed it down to around Southport or Preston.

So Smithy and I moved over into Southport. Though it's reputed to be a seaside town, you very rarely get to see the sea; there's more miles of sand than the Sahara. A good place to be based—medium-sized town and accessible easily to anywhere between Liverpool and Preston, with Manchester easily got at to the east—but not the sort of place you'd imagine for spies and sabotage. It's a retirement town, rich and stodgy, not so much Red Brigade as Blue Rinse brigade.

At one time the richest town in Britain, it's still very much upper middle clarse: perms, ballroom dancing, and poodles. Not, definitely not, spy country, you would have thought. Still … it's the surprises that keep you young, they say. So we packed our MOD-issue holdalls and decamped to Southport.

Which didn't turn out too bad. The Scarisbrick Hotel had a reasonable amount of totty—aging gracefully, or maybe disgracefully, but still looking good. And at least Smithy and I had separate rooms, which gave me hope of entertaining in peace. We placed our D/F vans at the ready: one on the Liverpool Road out in Ainsdale, one at Meols on the Preston side of town, and one out at Scarisbrick, on the Ormskirk road.

And we organised the local blue-pointed-head mob to pounce and arrest as soon as we got a fix. Smithy and I would, of course, be on the aggro team. Hopefully we would make a bust, then get a helicopter to wherever to forestall the next disaster. With us would go three SAS men pulled in from Hereford.

It's amazing what a bit of clout will do. No sooner had we decided a bit of hard-case backup may be needed and approached Whitehall than three long-haired pongos arrived post-haste, not long back from Northern Ireland, unshaven and dressed in cords, scruffy T-shirts, and desert wellies. All this laid on for a blasted antediluvian bit of wiggly Morse, when it takes Whitehall forever to answer my request for a new red pen.

Anyway, the three minders arrived: troopers Blair, Knowles, and Williams, or Ted, Alan, and Ken, as they preferred to be known. They all had, even in civvies, that quietly tough, competent demeanour of professional hard cases—so much more scary than all the bluff and bluster of dance hall bully boys. They were not unintelligent as pongos go; Ken in particular proved to be a likeable drinking companion and a reasonable partner in capurtle-hunting. Ted was a martial arts fiend and spent all his off-time hurling Smithy round a judo mat, whilst Alan spent all his spare time grubbing round second-hand bookshops.

We made an oddball quintet, but I suppose any five blokes in our line of work have to be a bit off-centre. And at least we worked well as a team, as we practiced assault techniques up and down the hotel's service staircase, to the bewilderment of staff and the annoyance of the management.

At last, the next D-day dawned.

Smithy was up while the lark was still snoring, as usual, jogging on the sand and practicing tai chi to the puzzlement and amusement of the local Pekinese-walkers. Then back to the hotel for his daily stint of cacophonous showering, praying, and Bible-bashing.

I asked him, "Smithy, lad, what do you pray about?" This time, I was sober.

But all he said was, "It's enough to practice the Presence of God, to be with Him, and to let Him play over my spirit. It helps make sense of my world. And of course, I pray for your black soul." All this said deadpan. It gave me the shudders!

Ken and I met over Alka-Seltzers and swopped lies about the blonde and her mate we had copped off with last night, whilst Ted lounged about with the *Daily Mirror* and Alan read his battered copy of J. D. White's *Genevieve* that he'd picked up for sixpence.

The day wore on slowly, grey and drizzly, our inevitable tensions building up. We strolled along Lord Street and down the beach road, chatting inconsequentially. We shovelled in steak and chips for energy in the boulevard restaurant. Gradually, talk grew terser and silences longer. I think we were all glad when it finally got dark, and we returned to the hotel to begin to get organised.

We all assumed dark clothing, and cleaned and loaded a Smith & Wesson .38 each. Smithy produced a nunchaku from somewhere and stuck it down his trousers. The local fuzz had provided an unmarked Rover 3500 and a town map. I drove, Smithy had the map in the front passenger seat, and the Three Wise Monkeys sat crushed in the back. We checked the radio links, got the D/F vans into position, and made sure Mugglesby were patched in and ready to record. Then we cruised gently up and down Lord Street like a kerb-crawler's night out.

11.58 Zulu. The tatty green unlettered J2 van lurched to a halt outside the Chinese restaurant. Two indistinct people in the cab. If a patrolling bobby saw it, it was just another protracted goodnight. The rear windows were blacked out, but the sidelights were on, and it was parked legally. No hassle, no suspicious circumstances, just a van and a courting couple, or a natter of pub-mates. All very innocuous.

11.59. A panel eased back in the roof. A long steel rod emerged.

00.01. The engine started, the steel rod withdrew, a satiated wasp-sting, and the van drove quietly and unhurriedly away.

00.01. The portable Army-pattern radio that Smithy nursed came to life. The groups came: NPOLI … GDIPR … OQKIT … ABYXS … IQRNO … repeated for thirty seconds.

00.02. The D/F coordinates came through: a Chinese restaurant on one of the side-streets off Lord Street. The hunt was on. We gently three-point-turned onto Lord Street and glided quietly to a halt outside the restaurant. No screaming cop-show skids, no whooping sirens, just a gentle pull-up with a quiet engine. The restaurant lights were out, but lights were on upstairs.

Out jumped the Three Wise Monkeys, S&Ws at the ready, and ghosted round the back to locate the rear entrance. Smithy and I sauntered casually up to the front door. Ten seconds' work with a credit card, and we were in. Careful creep through the restaurant and up the stairs, Smith & Wessons in hand, covering each other until we reached the landing and regrouped with the SAS lads.

Here we found another locked door—a mortice lock, so this time, the credit card was no good. Ken, six-foot-two of muscle, silently drifted up to the door and placed his gun in his pocket. He placed his hands, flat-palmed, on the door, knees bent. A quick intake of breath, a sharp expulsion of breath—*tchah!*—and the door slammed back against the wall.

In one fluid movement, Smithy broke right, rolled, and came up on his feet, gun out, covering the room. I leapt left to find and cover in a crossfire … a very startled Chinese couple sitting on a settee. Middle-aged, prosperous, well-dressed but tired, very obviously the restaurant owners, they stared, eyes rounded with apprehension and startlement.

"No money is kept here," said the restaurant owner, frightened but cool. "There's nothing for you."

As his wife's hand crept towards the phone, I shook my head and held out my warrant card. Smithy talked to them and went off to make them a cup of tea, while the rest of us went over that place like a Yorkshireman who's lost a shilling in there, but not a sausage did we find. Not a whisper of a radio receiver, not a secret compartment anywhere … nothing. Clean in fact. The flat was just what it seemed to be—a flat, and we couldn't make it anything else. We knocked on walls, pulled up carpets, turned out cupboards. It was clean.

The Chinese couple, restaurant owners as we thought, resignedly told us they hadn't heard anything unusual. Cars were always stopping and starting down that street, and they themselves were so tired after a busy night in the restaurant that I got the idea that a herd of elephants could have trooped the colour, complete with bagpipes, round the living room and they wouldn't have noticed. I wanted to rush off and start deciphering the letter groups we had intercepted, but Smithy insisted we put everything back just as it was before. Then wasted precious minutes apologising, out-Orientaling the Orientals. I expected him to start hissing through his teeth. "But no," he replied. "Only Japanese do that." All delivered with a straight face. I hazarded a guess he was joking, but I hate a smart-arse.

Finally, I ushered us out of the flat. Outside, on the pavement, Smithy's manner changed again, all brisk efficiency and steely-eyed determination. "Right, lads, we've got exactly ten hours and twenty minutes to find what is going down and where, and to get there."

George floated like a suffering, deluded Muhammad's coffin, but George floated between earth and hell. Consciousness began a long, limping climb to his brain centres. His body stirred; that war-burned, alcohol-burned body. His stiff leg twitched spastically, and its awakening ache cruelly coerced him into conscious thought.

He rose from his stinking army-surplus cot and lurched over to the sink. The sick smell of uncleaned drain hit him, and he vomited violently. Scrabbling frantically under the bed, amid the dust and discarded shoes, he found the half-bottle of Teacher's and gulped greedily. The raw spirit washed away the taste of sick from his mouth, brought his twitching limbs back into control, and anaesthetised his aching head. He lay back on his cot, still dressed in his once-fine sports jacket and cavalry twills, now stained with alcohol and sick, and hated himself.

So this was what things had come to. All the promise of his early years come down to this disgusting bedsit in inner-city Liverpool. His mind wandered ... the comfortable childhood in Surrey, son of a Harley Street surgeon ... the private education ... Cambridge ... the dashing young army officer, proud on horseback. The parades. The girls. The privileged but exciting life.

Then came 1939; the black, bitter tide sweeping over Europe; eventually rolled back, but at what cost!

The transfer to RAF bomber command as a desperately needed wireless operator. Berlin. Hamburg. Frankfurt. Dresden. Then the direct hit on No. 3 Engine over Darmstadt railway yards. The flames. The limp home. The crash landing. The year in Roehampton. George had been one of the unlucky ones: He had lived.

He had lived—if one could call it that—burnt, twisted, and disfigured. He had lived to be "rehabilitated" as useless, practically unemployable. After the war, he had worked on farms, in Northern mills, on the bins, until boredom, pain, loneliness, and the effect of his face on people made alcohol less of an occasional refuge and more of a constant necessity. Life demanded more and more alcohol, which demanded more and more absenteeism, until no one would employ him.

His embarrassed parents cut him dead. Who wants a burnt-bodied alcoholic around the place? The last twenty years had seen him become a hopeless alcoholic, lacking will or desire to dry out; lost to family, a progressively shrivelling leaf of a man, seared by the hot manic winds of the twentieth century—too traumatised to live, too scared to die.

And the uncaring juggernaut of the post-war twentieth century had brought him to this. This was Paranoia Day. Every month, the flames— orange, purple, acid-green, surely flames from the pit of hell itself. Back in the crippled Lancaster. The demons, black and faceless, hissing meaningless orders. And the Morse. Sending frantic groups. Ancient unpractised hand twitching, twitching ... surely this was hell. No real Hades could be worse than this.

Shakily, he reached out for the now-empty Teacher's bottle and hit it again and again, with weak, ineffective strokes, until it finally broke. He crossed himself, tentative and unpractised, then pressed the raggedly broken neck of the bottle against his left wrist.

And over in Presboro, the kraken woke. Disguised as a normal, rather pretentious middle-class woman, the alien woke up. Today was Vengeance Day. Smiling, she reached behind her dressing table for her transmitter.

And in London, a certain group in a certain embassy warmed up their transmitter as well.

Our next ten hours and twenty-one minutes made Bedlam seem a haven of tranquillity. Smithy herded us back to the car muttering, "A vehicle, it must be a vehicle." We imploded into the car and raced down Lord Street into Albert Road police station. There, in the room laid on for us, we frantically pored over the figures and a map, Smithy muttering, scribbling cabbalistically, drinking paper cup after paper cup of the station's Mersey-mud coffee, ruffling his hair, loosening his tie, and rubbing his eyes, until he looked totally demented.

Ted, Ken, and Alan calmly dismantled, cleaned, reassembled, and clicked their hand-weapons. I was straight away on a secure radio link to Mugglesby and Whitehall, setting up an open phone line; organising helicopter-loads of SAS, if needed; and coercing my reluctant masters into alerting every chief constable in the country.

At 3.30 a.m., Smithy produced the goods. It was … Liverpool. Here we were, chopper waiting on the sands, I phoning dementedly, prepared for a dash the length and breadth of the country, and the next excitement was to be fifteen miles away.

Sighs of relief all round. Relaxation. Loosening of limbs. A mental letting the braces dangle. Smithy looked up, stretched his arms, smiled like a Cheshire cat, and said, "Go and get the duty superintendent, Bill."

In no time, the duty super appeared—thankfully, a reasonably young, reasonably flexible, reasonably un-conceited man who expressed an enthusiasm to help.

"Now, Super," I said, "would you set us up a direct link to the Liverpool senior duty officer? We'll need every bobby and plain-clothes jack around the city centre. We'll need the chief fire officer alerted; we'll need fire crews on standby. The nearest bomb-disposal team. And would you put the Royal Hospital casualty department on standby? It might be an idea to get the Customs alerted, and especially the pier head for the Irish boats. And everyone warned of the dangers and importance of what we are trying to do. Speke Airport will need to be covered, and motor patrols on the A59, the East Lancs Road, and the tollbooths on the tunnel."

I continued, "We haven't worked out yet the exact location of the hit—Smithy hasn't broken that much of the code yet—but it will be city centre, and it will be an explosion. Both Lancashire and Merseyside chief constables have been notified by my boss at the Home Office and have given you carte blanche. So we leave it in your capable hands, Super, and thank you. We'll be at the Scarisbrick if you need us."

"OK, sir. I'll get you a driver to run you back. And I will, of course, observe strict secrecy."

"No to the driver, thanks, Super, the walk will clear our heads, but a very definite yes to the secrecy. Thanks again for your cooperation, and goodnight."

And so, anticlimax. We started with a tear-arse down Lord Street and the invasion of a Chinese restaurant and ended with a sedate stroll back up Lord Street. No one talked; we just breathed the predawn air and wondered what tomorrow would bring. We all thankfully collapsed in our pits and slept the sleep, if not of the just, at least of those who feel they have earned it.

Flight Lieutenant George Grayson dozed. Blood from his wrist turned tacky and sludgy. Booze-blurred eyes and whisky-shaking arms had managed to miss an artery. As he half-slept, half-drifted in and out of coma, he dreamed again.

Warmth flooded him. He chuckled. Boyhood in the Surrey countryside. Fox hunts. The army. The dash of a peacetime cavalry officer. He smiled as he dreamed of the time he had made a total ass of himself. He was dancing with a French countess of indeterminate age, but very determined origins, when he trapped his cavalry-sabre between his legs and fell down on top of her—cold sober—to the scandalised gaze of half the dowagers in the south-east.

But the dreams always ended in flames. First the excitement in the pit of the stomach and the ear-shattering roar of a thousand Lancasters lumbering into the sky, then terror. Falling and flames. Flames and falling ... falling ... falling. Crash onto Scampton runway. No longer warm, but terrified. Delirious, half awakened by the sound of knocking, he reached for the neck of his bottle and pressed it again and again in a lover's kiss against his wrist.

The knocking increased, crescendoed, and culminated in the door bursting open and slapping back against the wall. Three black-clad Mickey Mouses seized him ungently, saying, "No, Mucker! Not that way out. We still need you!" Rough, unfeeling hands bandaged his wrist with his own handkerchief, threw him back on his grubby cot, and flung, none too carefully, a crate of Teachers onto the table. The contempt was obvious in every syllable as Mickey One said, "Your wages, old man. Enjoy them!"

George wept, silently, shamefully, weakly as the broken door creak-slam-banged in the stairwell draught.

I slept dead to the world until nine o'clock, when I was dragged rudely and unwillingly awake by a shiny, freshly shaved Smithy leering down at me. He was dressed in cavalry twill trousers, Harris tweed sports jacket, blue shirt, and striped tie, looking every inch the senior officer.

"Come on, Bill, lad, show a disgustingly hairy leg. We've two hours to get to Liverpool. I reckon it's a bomb in C&A's."

"Urgghh ... wha' time d'you gerrup?" I enquired intelligently.

"I haven't been to bed! Someone has to keep the country running!" Smithy replied, grinning.

Ugh! One thing I hate more than a smartarse is a smartarse who's cheerful in the morning. While we five breakfasted delicately on the Scarisbrick's best bacon, eggs, fried bread, tomatoes, beans, toast, marmalade, and two pots of coffee, Smithy outlined the day's plans to us.

"The super managed all the official bits double-quick," said Smithy. "Smart guy that. But," he continued, "the store manager was a different kettle of fish. He was decidedly uncooperative at being dragged out of bed at five o'clock. So we gently reminded him," smiled Smithy reminiscently, "what a summons for negligence looks like, what bomb victims look like, what sort of reception his superiors would give his career prospects when it was reported in the *Liverpool Echo*, and what a bunch of litigious and possibly lynch-minded Scouse relatives would do to a guy who ignored an eight-hour bomb warning. He agreed." Smithy smiled benevolently.

What the store manager had agreed to was a "practice fire drill" at 11.00 a.m., with certain high-profile firemen milling around to add credibility and a low-profile bomb-disposal crew parked round the corner. At 11.15, with the main doors locked, the staff would look in all the obvious places for parcels, bags, coats—anything that could hold a bomb. They were told not to touch anything but report it immediately. At 11.30, the staff would leave and the bomb squad would take over. At 12.00, if we hadn't found anything and Smithy was right, there would be a bang big enough to feature on Granada news.

In the meantime, as of 10.00, there would be store detectives and plain-clothes policemen from the Liverpool force lurking, disguised as real people. They would trawl inconspicuously, looking at the bottom of stairwells, in cupboards, and under counters, while also looking for anyone abandoning plastic bags or holdalls worth making a lethal bang.

Now, being fully briefed and fed, I went to get my jacket.

"Right, Smithy, lad, let's go get 'em," I yodelled as I darted upstairs.

When I got down, Smithy already had the car keys and was heading purposefully towards the driver's door, but by making like a cross between Nijinski and the Great Houdini, I managed to nab the keys and fling myself into the driver's seat. I was ready to die for Queen and Country, but I didn't intend to be tortured by Smithy's driving first. Ken, Ted, and Alan climbed phlegmatically into the back, dressed in low-key civvies—flares, big collars, and bomber jackets—looking as innocuous as three psychotic gorillas.

We had a fairly gentle drive down the coast road to Liverpool. Usual corny jokes from Ken: "Eh, lads, I once had a one-legged girlfriend, but I told her to hop it."

"After that, you haven't a leg to stand on," grumbled Alan.

Smithy leaned over the front seat. "Can you lot not toe the line?"

"Now the boot's on the other foot," snickered Ted.

"OK, I acknowledge de-feet," I groaned.

We only had one bit of excitement when a noisy chopped Lotus Cortina overtook us on the Formby bypass: too quick, too close, and cut in too sharply. I swerved out at the Cortina—standard evasion tactics, at least by me—and felt the hairs on the back of my neck stand up as three sharp clicks came from the back seat. But false alarm. Only some young kid with more money than sense playing cowboys and Indians. He ranted off, exhaust snarling, never knowing how close he had come to him and his toy car being filled with 0.38-inch-diameter holes.

Other than that, we landed uneventfully in Liverpool, parked in Central Station car park, and strolled round to C&As just before eleven. The store was filled with middle-aged women and old wrinklies picking over the cut-price knickers and pottery gewgaws. And not one of them aware that but for a nosy RAF junior tech, most would be cats' meat within the hour.

We split up and began to merge with the shoppers. I thought my tweed hacking jacket and cavalry twill trousers blended in well—that is, until a store detective arrested me. Rather than make a fuss, I went quietly with her; she was a determined-looking blonde who had seen too much Emma Peel, but not bad-looking with it. I accepted arrest with as much grace as possible, not helped by Smithy and Alan smirking self-righteously across the counter.

In the manager's office, I explained who I was and flashed my SIS identity card. And even though time was a-wasting, I asked the lady shoplifter-lifter out for a date. Both my ego and my libido were shattered when she replied, "I'd love to. Mind if I bring my husband?"

Just then, the air was split with the hideous ululation of the fire alarm. This was confirmed when the tannoy announced, "This is a fire alarm. Please move quickly and quietly to the stairs, not the lifts. Repeat, do *not* use the lifts, and leave in an orderly fashion." After five minutes of eardrum-rupturing fire alarm, instructions-for-idiots, and stampeding customers, the store was quiet, the main doors were locked, and the staff members began earnestly seeking a plastic shopping bag, a holdall, a brown paper parcel, a bulky anything in a dark place or a rubbish-bin.

The staff girls moved in quick, jerky dashes from counter to counter, waste bin to waste bin, in a desperate effort to find a bomb yet stay alive.

After half an hour, the tannoy reasserted itself: "Will all C&A staff leave by the staff entrance; do not collect coats and personal effects but move quickly and quietly." The staff, with looks of relief and pretending not to hurry, scuttered out of the store like doe rabbits at the sharp end of a fox, leaving the store to the ministrations of the bomb squad, sniffer dogs, and some local bobbies.

The minutes crawled past, each minute winding the mainspring of tension tighter and tighter. Stress mounted on stress as the passing minutes failed to reveal any bombs. My hair horripilated as every step I took brought me nearer and nearer to eternity, or so I feared. I'd faced bombs before—and guns and knives—but you never get used to it.

At 11.50 and ten seconds precisely, a sniffer dog barked once, put his paws on an air-conditioning grill, and was detonated violently backwards, to wash up in bloody shreds against its stunned and by now handless handler.

The detonation brought us running, hearts pounding, throats dry, to find an unconscious policeman, uniform stained red from bits of his dog, bleeding profusely from the ragged stump of a hand where the one holding the dog's leash used to be. We slapped a tourniquet quickly above the stump, and his colleagues whistled up an ambulance pronto.

Smithy gazed down at the man so cruelly brought to the end of his career as he was wheeled away on a stretcher and went white. He was not a man who ever swore, but that brooding silence was more maledictory than any cursing. His face was wooden, his eyes blazed, and he breathed deeply three times. That was all, but somehow I knew that Smithy would move heaven and earth, or anything else in the way, to claim these characters. He turned on his heel and stalked out, pausing to say to the duty superintendent, "I want the store manager and maintenance manager in the office at two o'clock please, Super. Thank you."

Then he strode out.

I had a very shocked pie-and-pint in the Legs of Man pub with Ken, Ted, and Alan, and never saw hide nor hair of Smithy. When we returned to the store at two, Smithy was already there, now genial and expansive.

"We've got 'em now, lads. A real give-away!"

27

"Why?" Ted asked.

I answered, "No one can just walk up to an air-conditioning vent in a public store, undo it, and plug a dirty great lump of gelignite behind it. So it's got to be someone with access, bogus or otherwise, and he has to give a worksheet and invoice. And that's got to have a name on it. We're on our way!"

Already, the salvage-squad lads were beginning to scrape up the debris, so the store manager came over and introduced the maintenance manager and the security chief. And the local police inspector and his bagman came and introduced themselves. They led us up to the manager's office and presented us with a file of all the recent bills-of-work and invoices for work done round the building.

"You don't do your own air-conditioning, then?" I asked.

"No, the job's far too complicated for general maintenance men and too infrequent to keep an expensive specialist on the payroll, so we contract out."

In short order, we had it nailed. It wasn't the regular contractors, it turned out; a small outfit in Liverpool 8 had been subcontracted, and the job had been signed off only yesterday by what looked like *J Brady*, or *Brody*, or some such. We commandeered it. Smithy's avian features split into an evil grin as he made a big show of thanking the store personnel.

"Now, lads, a bit of a con job. Mr Manager, can I borrow a typewriter for a minute? Ted, Alan, Ken, take a stand-down. Take a couple of days off, and go back to your ever-lovings. Be back here Monday. Bill, you and I have a bit of play-acting to do. And tomorrow, Bill, I want you in jeans and a denim jacket. And don't shave tonight."

Smithy outlined the scam to bring Brody/Brady into the light. Then, sitting down at a typist's desk, I typed out an IOU for five big ones— £5,000, that is. Smithy carefully traced J. Brody-or-Brady's signature on the bottom and got the lot xeroxed. Satisfied, I folded it a few times, rubbed dust in it with a finger, and put it in my wallet.

The rest of the day was uneventful. We went to visit the Royal Hospital to find out the state of the dog handler. He was recovering "as well as could be expected" but was too dazed and full of morphine to say much. Smithy sloped off somewhere to get some things and have his hair cut, then we spent the evening in the Scarisbrick bar listening to a lady who could have been older and uglier just-sing old tired standards in an old tired voice. I had a couple of pints of Guinness; Smithy had a tomato juice.

Just before we bade our sober goodnights, Smithy said, "Don't forget, Bill, keep three paces back from the razor tonight. I want you looking even more villainous than usual, if that be possible!"

"Thanks, mate!" I recognised the compliment and grinned. Smooth talker, our Smithy.

4

NEXT MORNING, I DUG OUT THE OLDEST PAIR OF JEANS I HAD, A sweaty Beatles polo neck, my denim bomber jacket, and a pair of scuffed Doc Martens. I combed my unruly hair back with Brylcreem and put on a pair of shades. I looked in the mirror and shuddered. I have always been at the rougher end of the spectrum of male beauty, but this morning, I even gave me the shakes. I would hate to meet me down a dark alley.

I went down to Smithy's room and entered without knocking, and what a sight met me. He was, as usual, on his knees with his black book, but then he got up. His hair was cut in that neat, short, boxer look that the best criminals favour. Where on earth he found a shop open at this time of the morning beats me. His suit was a sharp Italian three-piece. His shirt was an immaculate white, and his tie was silk—a blood-red slash of colour down his front. His shoes were brutal-looking Oxfords, belooped with ugly-looking "diamonds". He looked like every successful gangster ever.

He grinned, looked me up and down, and said, "You'll do. Let's go and get breakfast and see what the other denizens of this caravanserai make of us!"

So we did. We breakfasted well, amused by the glances and cross-currents of *what is this place coming to.* No doubt we cost the hotel a fortune in return bookings that day.

Outside was a big black Mercedes 190. Smithy grinned at my surprise, threw me the keys, and said, "We've got to look the part when we go visiting." I drove fairly sedately to Liverpool, and Smithy directed me onto the dock road. We were heading for an address just off Parliament Street.

As we neared it, Smithy said, "Pull over. I'll get in the back."

He did so, and as we resumed our stately progress, he briefed me. "We're going to see the lie of the land—what's with the cowboy outfit that mended C&A's air-conditioning, Aqua Heat by name. But we don't want them to get wind of what we're about. Hence, the forged IOU. Leave the talking to me; just grunt if I call on you. Turn left up here—up the hill."

We caught sight of the target's premises. It was bigger than I'd expected, but still mostly front. I swept in the heavy wooden old-fashioned gates, heavily festooned with barbed wire, and parked with carelessness and panache right in the managing director's space.

I slouched out and opened the back door for Smithy, who got out looking a million dollars—all of them illegal. He stalked fastidiously across the wet concrete, paused regally while I opened the office door, and strolled insolently into the office, to be met by the radio asking us if we were going to San Francisco, and don't forget the flowers in the hair.

Smithy's disdainful gaze lasered round the room, resting finally on the teenage female werewolf on the switchboard. "Boss in?"

"Ew er yew?" retorted Dracula's daughter.

The ice burned in Smithy's eyes, and Medusa coloured and fumbled for the intercom. I reached over and switched it off, as Smithy panther-stalked to the inner door. He opened it and oiled in, stopping just inside to give, once more, his disdainful assessment. I stood just behind and to the right, knuckles trailing the floor, giving the office's rightful occupant a few kilowatts of menacing stare. He was a fat man, tastefully dressed in tan Crimplene trousers, green nylon shirt a size too small to meet over his fat belly, and a quizzical smile.

"Yes, gents, what can I do for you?" he smiled. But the smile froze as Smithy lasered him and I growled.

"Yew gotta fitter called J. Brody or Brady?" Smithy whispered in a mincing middle-class Scouse tone.

"Jim Brady, but why? Wozzit to do wit youse?" asked Office Dweller, beginning to take umbrage.

Smithy very slowly took out and unfolded the counterfeit IOU and let it fall disdainfully on the desk. "I have a friend who is offended when he sees that many noughts on a piece of paper. In fact, he is so upset that he asks us to come around and talk to that person. Isn't that so, Bill?"

"Urgh," I assented.

"So we really feel we must urgently talk to Mr Brady, to let him know of our client's discomfiture, that so, Bill?"

"Urgh," I repeated.

"Our friend does *not* like that much discomfort," minced Smithy. "He is quite upset. He wants us to have a quiet word with Mr Brady. In private. Is that not so, Bill?"

"Urgh!"

"Well," offered the Office Dweller, "he's not in today—hasn't been in since last Friday. He's sick."

"He will be," Smithy promised. "Very! Now, Mr ...?"

"O'Brian."

"... O'Brian, we need his address."

"Oh, I can't give you that," O'Brian replied.

Smithy stepped to one side, and I snarled and Neanderthal-ed forward, knuckles scraping the ground. O'Brian looked at us both and decided one fitter, and a poor loser at that, wasn't worth a thumping. He squawked into the intercom, "Daisy!" (Daisy yet!) "Bring in the personnel files!" Daisy came in with an armful of untidy files, put them down on the desk, and fled.

"Here we are, gents!" The joviality was back. "Sixteen Pleasant Place, Kirkdale."

Smithy produced a gold-capped pen and, fastidiously tearing a strip from Mr O'Brian's current order book, wrote down the address. He turned on his heel and stalked to the door, me following like a faithful psychotic Doberman.

Smithy stopped in the doorway, turned, and again lasered O'Brian. "Mr O'Brian, does your mouth unhinge easily?"

"Ur, no, I can keep stumm."

"Good, cos if word gets there before me, you'll need an enema to clean your teeth." And he swept out.

Smithy panthered across the wet concrete and stood by the rear door of the Merc as I fumbled the keys from my bomber jacket. As I bent forward, I received a push. I staggered and turned angrily round. There stood two boiler-suited Godzillas, one black, one white. Both were about six feet fourteen tall, both had faces like bags of hammers, both had massive steel-toecap boots, and both had biceps like ordinary people's thighs. Smithy oiled round the car boot like a greased cobra and stood to my right.

Joe Louis rumbled at me, "You leave Jim Brady alone. He's our mate."

Primo Carnera gurgled his assent, snarling like an Alsatian choking on a human leg.

I tried appeasement. "Look, lads, we're only doing our job. If he can't keep off the tables, it's not our fault."

"Dat's a downright piggin' lie," exclaimed Carnera hotly. "Two bob on de 'orses is 'is barra."

As he declaimed this, he seized me by the lapels, knee going for my genitals, and head butting for my face. I turned sideways, catching the knee on my hip bone as his head slid harmlessly past, then a quick flip with my right leg harnessed his momentum to land him flat on his back in the puddles. A quick stiff-finger poke on the neck left him sleeping Neanderthal-ly on the concrete.

I stood up just in time to see Number Two toppling like a stricken ebony tree whilst Smithy pirouetted gracefully around him. I looked round to see startled round mouths and eyes at every window.

"Right, Smithy," I said, "into the back of the car with them. Safe house for a few days."

It wasn't easy getting forty stone of unconscious Scouse into the car, but we managed and drove sedately away just in time to hear Liverpool City's finest banshee coming towards us. We parked round the corner, as Ratman and Bobbin started to stir noisily. Smithy produced from somewhere a brown bottle, poured some on a handkerchief, and gave them both a quick sniff. Peace returned to the car as they returned to the arms of Morpheus, and we set out to find a working phone—round here, as rare as an honest politician.

At last we located one, and I got out and contacted our Beloved Führers in the Great Wen.

"Right, Smithy lad, straight down the East Lancs Road and down the M6 to Keele Services. There we meet people who will look after Tweedledum and Tweedledee for us."

Smithy had sneaked into the driving seat while I was in the phone box. We kangarooed away as he asked, "Why are we taking them? Why not just dump them? They haven't done anything but show loyalty."

I sighed. Him and his scruples.

"Regrettably, we need to exert pressure from every side. And if two characters are seen fighting with two of J. Brady's friends after asking for him, and the friends disappear, that will get back to Brady and his bosses. Then maybe he'll make a mistake. And also, what if these two are in on the deal? They're better off out of the way for a while—a bit of a holiday for them. SIS will treat them well; as much Guinness and raw human flesh as they want, and eventually they'll turn up back in Scouseland with a few pounds in their pockets and a bad case of selective amnesia. Now shut up and pretend to drive."

Smithy sighed. "Yes, I suppose you're right. And now, I've got to repent of that violence and plan our next move."

See what I mean? Totally crackers!

Eventually, we reached Keele; uneventfully dumped the car with SIS; and drove back to Southport in a D-reg Viva. There we changed back into human clothes and plotted our next move.

5

NIGHT SHIFT. TEN THIRTY. I DOZED FITFULLY BEHIND THE WHEEL OF the Viva. Ken, Ted, and Alan were back in Southport, and the last few days had seen us taking turns boringly watching J. Brady's des res in the '30s-built Corporation flats, where he lived with his elderly Irish mother. Pleasant Place? Good to know someone on the Corporation had a sense of humour.

Fliers and phone calls to Liverpool City Police, SIB, Customs, and MI5 had produced a life history of J. Brady. He was suspected of being a minor criminal and a low-level IRA link—not politically minded, just bloody-minded. He had come to the attention of the Belfast law at 14, for shoplifting, and had progressed into gang warfare, stealing cars, and mugging. After he moved across the water, he had done time in Walton jail. He had been committed to Moss Side top-security mental hospital for a short while but had convinced the shrinks he was cured. He was now, to all intents and purposes, a sane and honest upright citizen, holding a job and going straight ... apart from his IRA connection.

Smithy conjectured, "This isn't likely to be IRA work; too quiet, too amateurish, and too unheralded."

"Yeah, it's frustrating that it's so ramshackle," I agreed. "It just doesn't feel IRA—so inefficient, and never any warning. But that isn't to say that the Fenian foot soldiers couldn't have subcontracted our spooky Morse sender."

I dozed while Smithy read his Bible.

We chatted idly.

"Smithy, why do you spend so much time reading that? Haven't you got to the end yet? Has the butler dunnit?"

"I read it because it's God's letter to humanity," he replied.

"But isn't it a bit old hat, all those *thees* and *thous* and *verilys*?"

"Not this one. This is an up-to-date version."

"Yes, but isn't it a bit childish and unbelievable? All those miracles? All those witches and magic and fairies?"

"Well, there's no magic or fairies, and precious few witches. But I've seen miracles—people that doctors have given up on healed by prayer. And I know that when my wife and child were killed, it was only this book and prayer saved my sanity."

The poor gook! Grief had been rationalised into the inscrutable ways of an unknown god.

I mentioned this possibility to Smithy, but he replied, "Not so, Bill. I've known God since I was 16, when a girl I rather fancied took me to church. I went there to be bored rigid, all *thou shalt nots*, organ music, and long boring sermons. But there I found life and excitement and friends, and a totally new take on life, as I gradually realised—oh, not very clearly at first—that God is real, that it's a great life, and I thoroughly rec ... but isn't that chummy over there?"

And sure enough, there was J. Brady slinking out of the flats like a ghost with a guilty conscience. I leapt out of the car with a cry of "'night, Harry!" and weaved along in J. Brody's wake with my Frank Sinatra pork-pie hat perched on the back of my head, singing softly that love is like a violin. As I passed another block of flats, I ducked in as Smithy cruised past in the car.

The student at the university left late. Work on her dissertation plus a quick Christian Union meeting in the uni bar meant she would have to hurry. She decided to take a shortcut through the Bullring, usually safe as anywhere in the 'Pool but sometimes a little rough. She was about three quarters through when, out of the shadows, lounged three spotty herberts. Being shapeless in a black duffle coat, she appeared to be a bloke, a student, and worth robbing.

"Okay, mate, let's see yer wallet!" Spotty One swung her round.

"Eyup, mate, it's a bird!" Spotty Two leered, leaning forward, "Gizza kiss, sweetheart! Ey! It's a *black* bird!"

"Tweet, tweet," carolled Spotty One, laughing at his own joke. "Come 'ead, Tweety Pie, first time I've 'ad a black bird." He put his arm round her shoulder. "Cummon in 'ere, Luv. OWW! Whatyer do that for?" He knelt on the ground, nursing a dislocated wrist.

Spotty Two swung a roundhouse punch at her head, a tactic that had won him many a scrap on the cobbles. Stepping to one side and turning sideways, she grabbed the incoming fist, wrenched it behind his back, and used his momentum to run him into the wall. She followed up running with him across the pavement and, with a quick flick behind the knee, dumping him alongside his groaning, swearing mate.

"'Ere, that ain't fair!" protested Spotty Three.

"Feeling left out?" she hissed, starting forward.

Turning on his heel, Number Three legged it into the shadows as fast as he could.

"Now listen carefully. And believe what I say," she said, panting slightly from exertion, fear, and adrenaline. With smooth, dark-chocolate, almost caressing tones, she purred, "Not so hard, are you, lads? But I know your faces. And if I hear up the road of any student being hassled, or even tripping over a paving stone, I will be back—and next time, I won't be so gentle!"

Spotty One groaned but nodded.

"Ey! That's not fair!" said Spotty Two. "We was only 'avin' a laff!"

"What's not fair?" she asked.

"Well, look at 'im!"

Thoughtfully, she said, "Yes, you're right. It isn't fair that he should suffer alone." And with a quick wrench, she dislocated Spotty Two's shoulder. "Together in everything, good mates, eh?" she added mockingly. "Now, I strongly advise you to get quickly round the corner to the Royal. But I would think twice about telling them you came off worst to a blackbird!" Trembling slightly but walking insouciantly, even whistling, she continued on her way.

J. Brady caught a No. 81 bus out towards Garston as Smithy picked me up on the next corner, and we played ducks and drakes with the bus till J. Brady got off. Then Smithy dumped the car on a double yellow line, and we followed on foot along the Cast-Iron Shore. As we left the shoreline into the maze of derelict, vandalised tenements and small businesses, I noticed we had a shadow. A tall, black-clad figure in a hooded duffel coat was following us.

"Tail!" I hissed at Smithy.

"The usual?" he asked.

"Sure!"

At the next corner, I hung back while Smithy still strolled on, talking interestingly about his newfangled washing machine. The shadow turned the corner. I reached for it, putting one arm around its throat. But before I could lean back, put the ghost on its back, and render it harmless, my ears rang to an eldritch shriek—*tchaah!* I found myself levitating six feet above Liverpool, which I soon rejoined with a bone-graunching thud. As I rose dazedly to my feet, I dimly saw Smithy close with the shadow, and there began the manic waltz of judo, suddenly ending in a flurry of limbs, out of which Smithy came on top.

Smithy hauled the figure to its feet as I pulled back the hood. "It's a girl!" I gasped intelligently.

"That's right, it is! And if you don't let go, I'll break both your bleeding arms!" snarled the virago in a Roedean accent.

But what a looker! Black, tall, with the proud features and upright carriage of the Masai framed in black, Western-style hair. And even through the duffel coat, noticeably stacked.

She opened her mouth to scream, so I clapped a by-now-dirty paw over it.

"Why were you following us?" Smithy asked.

"I wouldn't follow the likes of you—I've got better things to do," Roedean replied.

"Where to? Where from?" Smithy snapped.

"Nothing to do with you!" she snarled through my enveloping hand. "But if you want what I think, you've got a fight on! I've already dealt with one triplet of would be 'ard cases!" Still hyped after the Three Spotties encounter, she snarled and wriggled.

"Nothing like that," I growled. "This is official!"

"OK, dearie, promise not to scream, and my Neanderthal friend here will release you," Smithy said.

Neanderthal! A man of my good looks. Huh!

Anyway, I let her go, while Smithy very slowly and carefully, so as not to alarm her even more, pulled out his temporary SIB card and held it up to a street light for her to read.

"OK," she said, still trembly. "But why would our sleepless Guardians of the Peace want to duff up an innocent ethnic minority going home?"

It transpired that she had been kept late at uni at—of all things—a prayer meeting. *Not another one!* I thought. *If all these God-botherers fight like this one, I'm outta here.*

Immediately, she and Smithy went off into a sort of theological gobbledygook, which might have been Swahili for all I understood, she speaking through my hand, muffled but still viperish.

Smithy replied, "We were following a man suspected of blowing up C&As, but now we've lost him."

All the while, I was cringing, imagining being beaten to death by leather-bound copies of the Official Secrets Act. Smithy, ever the gallant, said we'd see her home and explain to her parents why she was showing up late and dishevelled.

"By the way, what's your name?" Smithy asked.

"Karen," she replied.

"Karen what?" I asked.

"You'll laugh," she said.

"We won't."

"OK, it's Karen White ... there! I knew you'd laugh! Anyway," she mocked, remembering the ID card, "John Smith is a pretty stupid name ... if it's your real one," she doubted waspishly. "You must have fun with hotel registers! And who's your gorilla mate?"

"Superintendent Bill Watson, fresh out of the trees, and right out of bananas at your service, Madam." I let her go and bowed. She had recovered enough to giggle.

"This really is not my night," she complained. "I had to deal with three real idiots up in the Bullring already, then you jokers turn up!"

We walked along, Karen and Smithy chatting, me bringing up the rear. It seemed that Karen was the child of a white ship's engineer, Henry White, and a Kenyan, unpronounceably named mother. She (Karen) had been brought up in Mombasa, going to an expensive girls' school, but had come to Liverpool with her parents to nurse her gran, Henry's mother, five years ago. She had gone forward and got "saved"—whatever that is—at some sort of religious nonsense in the Empire Theatre in '65. She now went to a small tin chapel down by the docks. She was 21 and a black-belt second dan in judo—martial arts and self-defence being one of the subjects taught to the daughters of gentlefolk in her genteel private school in Mombasa. She was doing a master's degree in education at the university.

As she thawed, Smithy was crowing with delight at her. *Smitten*, I thought. We reached her home and were ushered in to meet mum, a Masai princess like Karen who called herself Molly in England; her dad, a craggy, seafaring Scouse; and grandmother, a Giles granny with a Liverpool accent. We were sat down, forced to drink Glenfiddich and rank Scouse tea, and fed copiously on homemade cakes.

When Smithy explained what had happened—again with the tearing up of the Official Secrets Act—her parents, after expressing concern and "Oh Karen, do be careful," laughed uproariously with relief. Granny chattered on, "Half Scouse, half Masai, course she can look after herself!"

We mumbled sheepishly, embarrassed that a pair of hardened, experienced scrappers should have so nearly been bested by a student, and a girl at that.

"Ar, eh, our Karen, trust you to pick up a couple of sneaky-beakies!" said Henry, while Molly and Grandma just expressed concern, again, about Karen walking home through Liverpool 8.

"But as you see, Mumsy, it took two trained killers to get me. And even then"—with a sideways look at us—"they didn't do that well!"

Eventually, at about 2 a.m., we left to find our old D-reg Viva miraculously un-vandalised and drove the thing back to Southport. "Smashing girl, that" is all Smithy said, before lapsing back into a catatonic trance.

Next morning, I came down to breakfast moody, unshaven, and frustrated at letting Chummy get away last night, only to be faced with Smithy loping up the stairs in his tracksuit.

"Been jogging?" I asked intelligently.

"Yes, it's great, ran to Ainsdale and back. Beautiful morning. You should do some."

I repressed a shudder.

"OK," Smithy grinned. "Give me ten minutes for a shower and we'll discuss our next ideas." I sat in the dining room with my stomach rumbling Richter scale 5, fending off the geriatric waitress, and wishing Smithy's minutes were as short as normal people's.

Eventually, he appeared, charmed the old lass with the black dress and tray into producing two breakfasts that made Gargantua look like he was on a diet, and started straight in.

"I was ready for that!" Smithy sighed, replete. "Brody seems to be moonlighting without telling his IRA bosses. I reckon we can make him feel uncomfortable. So, after breakfast, go and put your hooligan's outfit on, and we'll pay him a visit. See you in your room in one hour."

An hour later, and once more done up in bristles, leather jacket, and denims, I lay reading an old Agatha Christie when there came a knock on the door and a vision of loveliness breezed in. Smithy's hair had been dyed red and slicked back. His jacket was Donegal tweed. He swung a stick. He limped. And finally, over his left eye was a patch.

When he spoke, he spoke not with the stage-Irish *begorrah* that we all know and hate but with the mincing preciseness of one born within the Dublin Pale.

We drove back to Liverpool. The old Viva would know its own way by now. Thankfully, Kirkdale was our side of the city, so I did not have to fight the town centre traffic with our old rust bucket. Ken, Alan, and Ted followed at a discreet distance in an equally disreputable Capri. They had contact with us by walkie-talkie, photos of Brady, and a Nikon with telephoto lens. They would park up in front of Brady's flat to await developments. We drove past the flats towards the Irish ferry, parked, and walked back. An IRA lieutenant would not be seen dead in a clapped-out Viva.

As we entered the portals of J. Brady's choice maisonette—avoiding the dog excrement, empty bottles, and puddles of human urine—I looked at Smithy. He no longer looked like a walk-on Irish comic. His walk had become a panther slide, heightened by the slight limp. His one revealed eye glittered, and if I had been RUC, I'd have arrested him on the spot.

As we reached the door, he nodded to me, and I gave a soft thump.

The door opened and a bleary ferret-head stuck out breathing halitosis and last night's Tetley's at us.

"Yer?" the face asked.

Without seeming to move, I pushed the door. J. Brady did a back somersault and landed on where he keeps his brain. He gawped at us.

Smithy stood over him, walking stick tapping menacingly in his hand. Brady's ferret-features changed from bewilderment to belligerence. He started to rise, making assumptions about Smithy's parentage. Smithy gave me a nod, and without a word I reached out a foot and swept J. Brady back onto his duff. After a further minute spent staring coldly and balefully at ferret-face, Smithy spoke.

"Mr Brady, iss it not," he hissed malevolently. "You have two sisters back in Belfast, Mr Brady ..." A further pause to demoralise Brady. Then ... "And Mr Brady, aren't you contracted to Us? Aren't you a True Patriot? Don't you care about Our Country? Are you not committed to a United Ireland?"

"Aye, sure, course I am," he mumbled defensively.

"Well then," Smithy went on, cobra-like, "Why do I hear of your moonlighting?"

Splutters from Brady.

"Sean!" Smithy rapped. (*Sean, yet!* I thought.)

Obediently, faithful old Doberman me picked up Brady with one hand and snarled, "Keep still or yer dead!"

Brady went red and then white and gawped meaninglessly. He did not look too happy. Smithy reached over my arm and tapped him in the chest. Brady, with his toes just touching the ground and his disgusting shirt bunched in my fist, just gurgled.

"Now Jim lad," Smithy drawled. "You're our boy. You belong to Us. Yet you've been a bad boy. You've been unfaithful. You've been moonlighting. That's very naughty. Plays tricks with your health."

All the time Smithy was talking, he was tapping J. Brady meaningfully on the knee with his stick. Brody, pale to begin with, achieved the impossible and went a whiter shade of pale. A hung-over Irish bum would not miss the allusion to kneecapping.

"Now," Smithy continued, "you must return to the fold. You must stop this prostitution. You have one aim, and that is not to make money or indulge in criminal acts. It is to Unite Ireland and free her from the Scotch yoke that the English have bound her with."

Then he had to spoil all that noble sentiment.

"And if you don't, I will guarantee you will never walk again! Sean!"

On command, I favoured Brady with my best King Kong snarl, shook him like the rat he was, and dropped him. Turning, we swept out with all flags flying.

Safely ensconced back in the Viva, we settled down to await events. Nor did we have long. Within five minutes, the radio crackled to life. Alan reported that a very scared Brady had scuttled ratlike out of the flats, The Capri joined in fairly cautious pursuit. We tagged along, two lorries back. Brody scurried along until he found a phone that worked. He had a long, expostulatory, and seemingly not-over-comforting conversation with someone. All Ted could make out with the binoculars was part of a local number.

Then, conversation over, Brody scurried back to his flat. Smithy went somewhere to divest himself of tweeds and red hair and came back in flares and T-shirt to settle down to wait. And wait we did, doing infinitely long, infinitely boring two-hour shifts in pairs.

Eight p.m. found Smithy and me on watch together again. I could not help needling Smithy about his religion, because the black book was very much in evidence again.

"How do you reconcile your Boss's attitude to peace and telling porkies, with the way you carried on this morning, scaring poor little ferret-features out of seven years' growth?"

"Yes, well ..." Smithy conceded, thoughtfully. "I do have trouble reconciling these things. That's one of the minor reasons I resigned from the Mob; I was beginning to like the violence, and my wife was starting to complain that I always came home looking like someone who had gone fifteen rounds with Henry Cooper. But here we are dealing with cruel and remorseless people who have been killing and maiming people quite casually—apparently for some time now. And I think that's even worse than putting the frighteners on J. Brady. In fact, I have set myself to deliver these people up to justice." (That's how he talked sometimes.)

He went on, "And to that end, I have committed myself. And if I am wrong, then I will apologise to my Boss. And anyway, I did not hurt him, only frightened him. And God loves everyone—even little rat-faces. But he doesn't always like what we do. Sometimes I need a lot of repentance, and my only excuse is that of damage-limitation: how many more people could be killed or hurt if we didn't do this? But I still don't find it easy."

I thought of the little fracas in the yard of Aqua Heat and refrained from comment. We settled down again, Smithy reading his something theological and me reading last night's *Liverpool Echo.*

At nine o'clock, just when all the non-alcoholics go out to the pub, Brady emerged again, dapper in black shirt, white tie, green Crimplene trousers, and brown moccasins. What followed was a rerun of the night before, ending up past where we had met (met?) Karen White, in a wasteland of old tumbledown warehouses. We followed Brody at a very discreet distance. He was jittery, and one hint of a tail would spook him straight back home.

When he stopped and waited, we lurked a hundred yards away, having climbed to a first-floor window of a derelict warehouse, Smithy viewing him through the infrared night-sight of the Nikon. Once again, we waited.

After about an hour of cramp and boredom, we saw Brady jump. A Shadow had joined him. There was a brief altercation; Brady seemed to be pleading with Shadow. He plucked the man's sleeve, but suddenly Shadow turned and struck out. Brady fell, and Shadow stalked off.

Smithy gabbled urgently on the walkie-talkie, and we set off in hot pursuit of Shadow. At first, we tailed him leapfrog, Smithy in front, then me, with the other about fifty yards back. Then when Shadow turned onto a major and well-lit thoroughfare, we followed quite openly, arguing amiably, in the sententious manner that drunks do, about football and wives and politics. Somehow or other, Smithy also managed to shoot off a few infrared frames of the Nikon. As we turned off the main road onto a much narrower and darker road, we fell silent again and dived into a flat doorway as Shadow turned to give the street the once-over. Then he darted away again. As we emerged to follow, we heard, "Well, look here, lads, a pair of poofters. Might be a bob or two on 'em, too."

Three would-be Jimmy jackety Deans stood right in front of us.

"Come on, youse, yer wallets!" snapped leather number one.

Smithy and I both sighed. Reaching towards my inside pocket, I cringed. As Spotty Number One leaned towards me, I brought my elbow into sharp contact with his spotty chin, at the same time hooking his feet from under him. As I did so, I saw Jimmy Dean number two flying past me at head height. I turned towards Jimmy number three, only to find him firmly in Smithy's grasp. Quickly, I whipped out our regulation cuffs and fastened the three together like a daisy chain round a lamp post, whilst Smithy once more muttered into the walkie-talkie.

Then we raced after Shadow. But no good. The black Liverpool night had swallowed him. I let out a string of curses which should have turned the Three Spotty Musketeers into charred bacon. Smithy merely smiled, but not pleasantly, and said, "Satan will have his little jokes, won't he."

We radioed Ted to pick us up, and we all somehow squeezed into the Capri. Ted, Ken, and Alan had decided not to involve the local fuzz with the three eejits—too much time, trouble, and paperwork—but had given them a thumping and a frightening and let them go. More seriously, they reported that ferret Brady had gone down his last rabbit hole. Shadow had killed him with surgical neatness by stabbing him in the peritoneum with a mass-produced, fingerprint-less kitchen knife, left sticking obscenely out of his stomach.

Retrieving the Viva, we drove moodily back to Southport. Smithy was having a fit of religious remorse and did not snap out of it even when I told him that his own black book said that those who live by the sword would die by the sword.

"It's at times like this, Bill," Smithy said dolefully, "that all the dressing up and the play-acting lose their exhilaration. A lie told by me sent that man to his death."

"I can't see ferret-features being a great loss: petty criminal and legman to not one but two bunches of terrorists, a very small cog in two scummy machines," I put to Smithy, but he rabbited on about Brady's lost immortal soul.

"I reckon that if Brady's got an immortal soul, he doesn't deserve to have it," I replied cynically. Which was no comfort to Smithy, who relapsed into gloomy silence.

At least we got back to Southport before the hotel bar shut. Smithy crawled back to his room while the Three Wise Monkeys and I sank a few pints to wash away the taste of Liverpool's decay, eyed the talent, and moaned at the fact that Shadow had got away. No doubt Smithy would say the devil looks after his own.

6

For two long days, Smithy sulked in his sweat-stinking room, not even emerging for meals. And when we looked in on him, he was sitting cross-legged on his bed, hair tousled, unshaven, face pale and sweaty, and eyes unnaturally bright. He looked like something no self-respecting cat would be seen dragging in. When we tried to talk to him, he smiled like his mouth was being stretched with fish hooks and said, "I'll be all right, lads, don't worry."

Finally, I got fed up with his poncing around, his principles, and his self-centred *poor old me*. "Come on, Smithy, lad. Get over it!" I snapped. "If this is having principles, I thank anyone who's up there to listen that I haven't. They cost too much and cause too much grief. Get your act together, get your skinny bum off that bed, and sort yourself out! We've got work to do and can't be fussing around while you come to terms with this! Think of all those dead on the trooping flight! Think of a handless copper! Think of the rest of us with our thumbs up our bums and our minds in neutral waiting to get on to Shadow! Go and have a shower, you stink!"

"You're right, Bill, forgive me," he answered wanly. "It was a bit egocentric, wasn't it? Give me an hour, and I'm with you."

After a long discordant shower of repentant hymns, Smithy emerged, pale but brisk, in his tracksuit; pounded up and down the Promenade a couple of times; and ate up what seemed to be the hotel's whole ration of breakfast. Give him his due—it might seem all brown rice and tofu when he's in Whitby, but here on the other coast it's all bacon, eggs, kidney, and loaves full of toast. And the sickener is, he still looks like a racing snake.

After making a pig of himself, Smithy ushered us up to his room for a council of war. "Right, lads. I've apologised to God for that monumental pig's ear."

At that point Ted chose to ride into the valley of death. "Is your boss deaf that it takes two days, or were the lines engaged?"

Smithy turned his head. He sighted his twin lasers on Ted and said very quietly, very conversationally, "Ted, please don't—not ever—make cracks about God in my hearing, and don't barge into things you don't understand."

Ted seemed ready to bite back, but a kick on the shin shut him up, and he mumbled a sub-aural apology. Just as well. Ted may be SAS trained, but the dark side of Smithy is something else.

So I took over. "Now lads, we don't really know what to do next. Shadow could by now be anywhere, but I've a feeling he is reasonably close—in Liverpool 8. Twice Brady went down to that area, and when we followed Shadow, he walked; he didn't seem to have driven to meet Brady, and he never looked for a cab or a bus. So he's most likely local talent. He's got a name, he must have a pad, and a big ugly dude like that must be known. Next: what do we do?"

At this point, Smithy put his oar in: "Easy. We recruit Karen."

The way Smithy said *Karen* showed me he had gonads like the rest of us. But I hoped his fine-tuned objective, if sometimes objectionable, brain wasn't going soft. When I put this to him, instead of brazening it out, making salacious comments, or even blushing as a flesh-and-blood person would, he just said, "One of the spin-offs of the prayer and meditation you take the mickey out of is the ability to be objective. She impressed me greatly, but at the moment she just may have the knowledge we need. She's local, she's black, and she's tough—as you know, Bill."

Did he have to remind me?

"So I'll go and see her today, straight after tea," he concluded. Of course I believed in Smithy's objectivity as I noticed the pigs cruising overhead. Note: *"I'll* go and see her," not *we'll.* Objective? Yeah! I still reckon he's fancying, and to hell with the Official Secrets Act. As my old dad used to say, "A woman will drag you farther than dynamite can blow you."

We spent the rest of the day slopping around collecting some enlarged copies of the dark grainy photographs that Smithy had taken of Shadow, teleprinting others to be distributed among the beat-bobbies and pandas in Liverpool 8, and resting. Then, after tea, Smithy appeared, spruced up, wearing smart tan slacks, desert wellies, smoothy shirt, and aftershave—aftershave yet! He took the keys of the Viva and spluttered off, driving the car along the white line like it was a monorail. As I've said before: Smithy's driving …

He came back after midnight, just when I was beginning to worry about the Viva. He looked exhilarated and pink.

"Takes a good few hours to look at a few mugshots!" I smirked.

Smithy, elated: "It was her Bible-study night, so I went along. And afterwards, to her parents' flat for coffee."

"Bible study and coffee! Smithy, what a wild, decadent, reckless devil you are!" I grinned.

Smithy smirked. "Anyway, Bill, the good news: as you know, Karen's at university, and as of Monday, they are on vacation. So she has promised to take me about each day to see if we can turn up Shadow."

Ken, Ted, and Alan sang quietly, "Young lurve, first lurve, te-tumte-tum, deep devo-shi-on."

Once again: *me*, not *us*.

"And the rest of you, or youse, as they say where I've just been," said Smithy, pretending to ignore us, "take two weeks stand-down. Then it'll be time to plan our next reception committee for our Morse-sending spook. And, er, incidentally, I'm moving into Henry and Molly's spare room, just to be on-site!"

And he's being objective?

Ted, Alan, Ken, and I disappeared about our various businesses—Ted and Alan to unlikely and child-strewn domestic bliss on the married patch at Hereford, Ken to chat-up some bird in Alnwick, and me … well, after a diligent bit of phoning, I was off to the Smoke to stop Vanessa getting frightened while her flatmate was away. I caught the next train at Lime Street and Nessie at Euston.

As always, when not being tousled by me, she looked cool and superior—lady-executive written all over her, knee-length skirt of severe black business suit, high heels, white tailored shirt showing off contours better than an OS map. Lust flowed through me like a Severn-bore of burning petrol, and the twenty-minute taxi drive wound me up to the pitch of a G-string.

The next fortnight passed blissfully enough, and I didn't spare much thought to how a religious-maniac stork and a judo-champion Masai princess were getting on, either in hunting Shadow or any other way.

Nessie and I get on well together. Whilst we weren't madly in love or anything, we liked each other, friendly as well as lustful, and enjoyed each other. Vanessa worked as a buyer in one of the posher chain stores. So she diligently went off at 8 a.m. every day, returned at 5.30, and allowed me to blunt her business efficiency from then on. After the tension of being wound up in stuffy radio rooms, the boredom of keeping watch on grubby flats in scabrous dockland, witnessing a murder, and the frustration of all the dead ends, it was a winding down par excellence, and my backbone and psyche alike felt the knots coming out. London had a few good folk clubs which we frequented, a lot of very good restaurants of all nations, and a few good shows. But all good things, as the cliché has it, come to an end, and Thursday night the phone rang: Smithy.

"Bill, you old son of a wondering sailor, time to drag yourself from the fleshpots of the Great Wen. Your country needs you. And so do I! Get over to Euston and get your reluctant ugly self back up here. Karen and I will meet you off the 7.48 at Lime Street."

Umm, I thought, *Karen and I, huh?*

That night was a fairly long, not entirely unemotional, goodbye to Nessie, then a long, dragged-out day until train time. A quick whisk up the North West route on the express, and I found myself and my luggage decanted onto the cold concrete of Lime Street Station. And there were Karen and Smithy, hand-in-hand. But as we got into the Viva, which had miraculously surviving a fortnight of Smithy's driving, it was all business.

"We think we know who Shadow is," Smithy began. "A cousin of Karen's lives in the same block as a Polish plug-ugly with a mile-long record for GBH, called Kowalski. And sure enough, he's a fair match for Shadow. He's fortyish and came over after the '56 uprising as a young man. He works, when he can be bothered, as a bouncer and enforcer. He has got form for minor offences, mostly affray and GBH, but don't forget also some of those refugees are suspected of being sleepers. The KGB likes to use Poles because most Poles are strongly anti-Russian and fit well into British culture."

Noticing Karen nodding eagerly, I asked, "What about the Official Secrets Act?" It was OK for civilian Smithy, but I was still on the Home Office's strength—and very accountable. And I would need a pension.

"It's all right," Karen answered. "John has had me sworn in as a special constable, and I've signed the Official Secret thingy as well."

That Smithy; he doesn't do badly in the miracle line. I can just imagine my boss, Sir Lindsey Attwaller, if I'd asked for Nessie on the team. And I've worked faithfully for him for years.

We drew up outside a dingy little pub somewhere along the dock road and went in. The noise and smoke hit us like a slap in the face, a stripper gyrated vacantly on the bar top, and all around us the stock market of the black economy conducted its manic business at the top of its voice. Smithy yelled, "Kowalski should be in about nine; you can get a look at him then. In the meantime, quick drink, and will you go and pick up the lads? They'll be in to Lime Street at about 8.30."

From the Sass lads arriving together, I gathered that Ken had not managed much in Alnwick. Hence, after a quick draft Guinness, I found myself on the road back to Lime Street. Surprise, surprise—their train wasn't more than five minutes late, decanting our three hard cases disguised as people, and from the uxorious look of Ted and Alan, home comforts must have been good. And from Ken's disgruntled air, Alnwick maybe not so good.

After a quick *How are you?*, *Good leave?*, *Great, you?*, we were on our way back to Seedsville. We cut our way in through the dark, the noise, the sweat, and the tobacco smoke ... with a whiff of other smoke. Smithy and Karen were tête-à-tête—impervious to us. They didn't hear us coming, and eavesdropping proved easy.

"But why not marriage?" Karen asked.

"Well, love, I'm a lot older than you. Nearly twenty years."

"Poor old man. I'll push your bath chair."

"But you need a lad your own age. What about the university students?"

"Wimps and wallies."

"Or local lads?"

"Yahoos."

"But what about ...?"

"John Smith." Karen's eyes slitted, and I saw why Africa had been so hard to colonise. "Are you sure it's not because I'm black and you're ashamed of me?" Lions looked out of her eyes. "Are you just using me as a buckshee sneaky-beaky, cos if you are, I'm out of here, and out of your life." She burst into tears.

"Darling, I wouldn't care if you were purple with pink dots."

An imperious lift of a black, very determined chin. "Well then?"

I never thought I'd see Smithy's lasers waterlogged. His eyes filled with tears.

"Well then, Karen White," he stuttered, "if you can put up with me, will you marry me?"

"Of course I will, you blind honky! And at least this way, I get rid of that embarrassing name of White!"

At that moment, I felt it polite to cough and ease forward.

"Bill, Ken, Ted, Alan, can I introduce you to ..."

"The future Mrs Smith," I completed.

"You heard."

"A bit."

After the proper congratulations, Ted fought his way through the gloom for pints for us and Cokes for Smithy and Karen. Then business.

"The large white man with the moonscape face leaning on the bar. That's Kowalski."

Kowalski was dressed in the dockside chic of donkey jacket, denims, and steel-toecap boots. He was massive, easily topping Smithy's six foot one, with a chest like a barrel, and his hands were huge. His hair was unfashionably short, and his face was red with alcohol abuse and incipient heart trouble, but he still looked savage—dangerous as sweating dynamite, and as unpredictable.

The Sass were too streetwise to turn and gape, but over the next few minutes, we all managed to fill our eyes and memories with the bitter silent man at the bar. This was a rough pub, full of hard cases, black and white, but Kowalski had a sort of wild-bull aura that even in this crowd ensured him elbow room. A dangerous man and one it wouldn't do to put a foot wrong near. Yet we were another step further, and if this was him—and it was so far only supposition—then we were that much nearer.

Smithy was talking again.

"So, we have a week before our next disaster scene. And this time, we'll get 'em. Up to now, we've just let the local fuzz keep an occasional eye on Kowalski, the beat-bobby past the front door, just spot but don't approach. This one's nasty.

"Karen and I have become established here as regulars, and his phone is bugged. But from now on, we sew him up tighter than a Scotsman's pockets. I've put in a bit of groundwork with the local CID. They can't use local faces, too easy to make, but they're bringing in teams from Manchester and Preston, and we'll handle this so carefully we'll make a falling feather sound like an explosion.

"You four won't be seen in here after tonight. You're booked in at the Scarisbrick again, twenty miles out of mischief, so that on D-day, you're our ace in the hole. Meanwhile, Karen and I will be seen in here most nights, and we'll meet as usual in the Scarisbrick daily for a Chinese parliament. And we've a lot of organising to do between now and next week. Not to mention breaking the good news to my prospective in-laws, or out-laws. So, drinking up time, see you tomorrow. Goodnight and God bless."

For the three Sass lads and myself, it was a fairly enjoyable week. We found a licensed martial arts club locally and practised most mornings. That was a sweaty time: the SAS train their lads well, and some of the local housewives were quite useful too—on the dojo, you understand, though one or two looked liked they'd be quite useful on another kind of training mat. Then in the afternoon, a quick swim in the Victorian indoor municipal pool, into the bar in the evenings, putting back the calories we sweated out earlier.

We also found time to relax—Alan grubbing around the local second-hand bookshops, the rest of us lounging, walking, eyeing the talent, and resting. And of course, Smithy coming out and briefing us every day. He was as busy as a fly in a tripe shop.

Then the final briefing, 5 p.m. Friday. "I've gambled on another local venue for our Morse-ghost," Smithy reported. "And I reckon it must be a vehicle. We turned over that area and that restaurant in Southport pretty thoroughly, and it wouldn't take much to put a transmitter in a car. Thirty seconds of letter-groups, then melt into the background. You'd need a biggish aerial, but in this day and age of radio-hams, you'd never even notice an aerial on a car."

"So what are we going to do?" asked Ted.

"What do you reckon to this?" Smithy asked in return. "Now we know roughly how they work, maybe we could fake a transmission just before midnight putting them somewhere believable without putting anyone local in danger, then immediately sending a gobbledegook of jamming—maybe Russian, as they are near that net—so the real message can't get through. We can maybe lead them into an ambush and bust the lot of them."

Smithy had briefed me on his loony idea previously, and we had discussed the feasibility and put in a bit of planning. But SAS have a long history of discussion before raids, and we wanted their commitment and enthusiasm. They were the experts in these sorts of under-the-radar battles. They had the technical skills needed.

So we discussed: where would be a good spot, weapons needed, what about police involvement, vehicles. In the end, we reached a working model. Place: an old Fleet Air Arm station near Burscough, quiet rural situation, poorly padlocked, with various small businesses in the old Nissen huts but ideally a long-distance haulage company big enough and important enough to be a target, and far enough out of the way not to cause any locals problems.

We would be in two cars—old bangers and parked round the back of the hangars. Weaponry would be flash bangs—acoustic and flash grenades—plus each with his favourite handgun and short-barrel Uzis. The local fuzz would keep to their usual patrols, but there would be armed response units with them. Smithy thought that this might be a bit of overkill, but the SAS insisted that all the best plans had a plan B to fall back on.

"Then we'll at send our disinformation at 23.58, followed by three minutes of Russian," he concluded. "Hopefully we'll get the foot soldiers and a clue to our ghost. Then hopefully, we will get an ID on the ghost, and we need to find out why, and then, hopefully, we are on the way to stopping—once and for all—this apparently random and useless killing, crippling, and damaging."

Then Smithy laughed self-consciously. "Sorry, lads, I'm on my hobby horse again." But by now, the guys were comfortable with Smithy's eccentricity and just smiled.

We laid our trap. Using my totally illegal set of picklocks, I picked the airfield padlock, then carefully relocked it after myself. We didn't want any giveaways for this fly mob to pick up. Out of courtesy, we had informed the haulage company owner that we were using his area for a Special Forces exercise, to keep him and his lads far away. We assured him no harm would be done to his premises. (*Hopefully*, we thought.) Dressed in dark clothing, flak jackets, and balaclavas, we lurked. Thankfully, there was no moon.

At two minutes to midnight, Smithy woke from his prayer-catatonia and pressed the tape button for the code, then the transmit button. Thirty seconds after, the tape spewed out booming Russian chatter that we had liberated from Mugglesby. Then we waited.

Two a.m., there was a quiet rattle as the gate chain was picked, and a shadowy van cruised quietly up towards the parked haulage trucks.

But something spooked them. The van screamed 360 degrees and ranted off. A back door opened and a pile of coltraps—spiked blocks—were scattered across the gate. Lights off, the van disappeared towards Southport.

Frustrated, the lads and I swore long and loud, and even Smithy snarled. Tiredly, we picked up the coltraps, loaded them in the Capri's boot, and dejectedly drove home, the lads off to the Scarisbrick, Smithy and I back to Karen's.

"I reckon those guys have supernatural powers," I half seriously grumbled. "What did we do to spook them?"

"Yeah, we were so careful. And I don't reckon they could see us, not where we were," said Smithy.

"Maybe one of us twitched. But for sure, this lot are super-alert, eyes and ears like sewer rats, and they can jump like hyperactive kangaroos. Now they know something's gone wrong, they'll be even more circumspect. Expect trouble. Especially you and Karen in that Liverpool 8 dive."

She was alone. She ranted, raved, and screamed—gutter language in English, Polish, and German. She stamped around. What in the name of anybody and everybody did that Polish oaf think he was doing? Telegram from him: "Order unsuccessfully delivered. Suspect rival firm."

She shrieked the harder, throwing herself on her bed, pounding the pillow with angry fists and kicking her legs. After five minutes, she calmed down, swallowed two of her prescribed pills, and washed them down with a hefty slug of Teacher's whisky.

If I can't trust that Polish oaf to get it right, I'll have to get rid. Uncle Bulgaria will need to expedite, she thought. *My brain is getting fuzzy. Not long now before this disgusting disease takes over, but I will strike at the fat cats. And it it's not syphilisnotsyphiliscan'tbesyphylis …*

She committed a cardinal error. She was alone. She warmed up her ramshackle transmitter, tuned into the frequency, and screamed at the Polish oaf, "Where are you? What are you doing about my order? *Answer me!*" She knew his tape recorder would pick it up.

We dejectedly stood the three lads down and sullenly drove back to Mugglesby, to be met by the welcome of, "I thought you'd finished here. How much longer are you going to be?" from a very disgruntled CO.

"Yeah, sorry, Wingco," Smithy apologised. "We had hoped to stop pestering you too. But unfortunately, something didn't pan out to our plan last night, so I'm afraid we're back. Let us take you down into Slagford for lunch, and we'll try to explain—as much as the powers-that-be will let us."

Brightening slightly, the CO agreed, and in no time flat we were ushered into the Station Humber Hawk and wafted into the best hostelry in Slagford. Guess a clapped-out rusty green Viva was beneath the dignity of the station commander of an important intelligence base. Under the benign influence of a large 21-year-old Laphraoig, the Wingco proved quite an interesting raconteur. He was not long back from a posting in Aden and was quite amusing on the inefficiencies of both the British and the terrorists, and interesting on the subject of the character of the army CO in Aden, Colonel "Mad Mitch" of the Argylls.

"A crazy jock in charge of a bunch of crazy jocks" was his summation. "And the sooner we get out of that fly-ridden sandpit, the better."

But all too soon, it was back to the old routine of searching the Russian net in case Matey changed his timing. This time, we were only allowed one W.Op.Spec per shift, and that very begrudgingly. We could hardly blame the station watch officers. "Need to know" was the rule, and we couldn't show any results as far as they were concerned.

We hung out in our smelly little side room and went over and over all the intelligence we had gathered until our eyes burst and we were losing the will to live. But we had one success. Quite by accident, the watch operator, who thankfully was Paul, picked up a burst of voice across the net, screaming in Polish and berating someone for failing to deliver the order.

We pounced on it with effusive cries, but not having any D/F, we couldn't tell where it was from, and reception was so poor we couldn't make out male or female operator. But it was a break in the gut-crushing boredom. So to celebrate, we put the kettle on and sent Paul to Slagford for doughnuts.

Kowalski got in from a gentle spot of protection racketeering and noticed the receive light was on. "That blasted Lady Muck again," he sighed resignedly, listening to the diatribe. "She is a pain in the butt, but as long as she keeps the chain golden, the bull will keep chained. For now!"

He took out his emergency contact phone number and rang.

"Get off the line, you idiot," she hissed. "He's home. Keep near your phone. Ten minutes." Putting her coat on, she cried, "Nipping down to the shops, dear!" and exited.

Kowalski's phone went. *Let it ring for a bit,* he thought. *Kowalski's nobody's lapdog.* Finally picking it up, he was greeted by a screech of gutter invective, strange from such a would-be posh scion of the local bridge club.

Finally, he got a word in. "We had no signal," he lied. "Reception was impossible. I was just about to ring you."

"OK, but don't let it happen again!" she snapped and rang off.

Sure, he thought. *I am really trusted, I have command even over airwaves! But at least she believed me. If I can lie successfully to Nazis, Russians, and the effete British authorities, she's no problem.*

As the time got closer to the next transmission, we moved back up to the North West. We met back in the Scarisbrick, including Karen, and got the lads back from Hereford. Thankfully, their Head Shed was cooperative; a big problem with a peacetime army is keeping them all busy.

We scrounged an easel and an A1 pad and produced a timeline. It had been over a year since Paul had first contacted his watch commander, and there had been numerous attacks, and we were not much further on. We kicked ideas about, discussing every possible and impossible scenario of why Burscough had gone wrong.

Finally, a red-faced Ken muttered, "I think I moved early; came out of the shadows too soon. Sorry, lads! Not very professional!"

Alan and Ted snarled at him for being a useless bag of fertiliser, but Smithy said, "OK, Ken, be a bit more careful next time, and you two get off his aching back! It's done! Can't undo it!" Grumbling, we settled down to plan.

"I reckon we'll employ the KISS principle: Keep It Simple, Stupid," I lectured. "Hopefully they'll think last month was just a hiccup and continue the mixture as before. We'll be on alert at D-Day H-Hour, and be on *total* alert." Smithy isn't the only one who can be pompous. The lads jeered and catcalled. Good. It reunited them.

"I've got a platoon of your mates up in Hereford on standby, which will be able to deploy anywhere at nil notice," Smithy continued. "The Head Shed seems to think it'll make a good training exercise. We're going to do the usual with the D/F—three D/F vans again, one at Ainsdale, one in Meols, and one in Scarisbrick. Bill and I will be in the Capri here outside the hotel with a receiver.

"I've also alerted the local blue-pointed-head mob here in Southport to keep a very strict eye open for big aerials, to report but not follow. I've a feeling those characters may be very alert and very dangerous, especially after last time, and I don't want any dead or injured bobbies on my conscience. And at the same time, you Three Wise Monkeys will, very carefully, follow Kowalski. Because if he is who we reckon he is, he's going to be in on the action. And while I don't want you, Karen, back in that pub alone, would you keep visiting your cousin to keep an eye on Big K?"

"*Jawohl, mein Führer,*" she smirked.

Look out, Smithy-boy! The future Mrs Smith will not be a doormat.

He grinned at her, but I could see Smithy was taking it even more personally. And I feared for the ghost. I only hoped there was enough of him left for us to interrogate.

Karen reluctantly went back to Liverpool. The rest of us went over and over the plan—if you could call it that. Then we scrounged a transit van that the Southport fuzz had impounded, and at dead of night, practiced attacks in the station car park.

The witching hour approached. The five of us crouched round the portable transmitter in the Viva like a bunch of vultures. Dead on time came the letter groups, Smithy scribbling cabbalistically, muttering insanely, and ruffling his hair. By 00.19 he had it.

"After all our nationwide preparation, it's just up the road—Ainsdale!"

"Right lads," I barked. "Ted, Ken, Alan, into the Viva, and off to Liverpool. You'll find Kowalski's address on the passenger seat along with an A-Z. Be very, very careful. Kowalski's a nasty bit of knitting and will be very, very fly. Before you get chez Kowalski, clock in at the main nick; they'll then alert their watchers, ID you thugs as on the side of the angels, and give you three cars to leapfrog. Kowalski won't—hopefully—smell a tail. He's got an old Austin Cambridge, reg. number on the clipboard, and I reckon if he goes anywhere, it'll be by car. See you later, lads, and God bless."

Ken, Ted, and Alan grinned like wolfhounds and loped upstairs to get changed. When they came down, they looked ... different. Dark polo-necked sweaters, black tracksuit bottoms, flak jackets disguised as body warmers, and carrying photographic gadget bags. In these bags were balaclavas, black gloves, a stripped-down Uzi sub-machine gun each with spare magazines, a ten-inch commando knife each, and a tube of black camouflage cream. They were also each carrying, in bizarre contrast, a dirty fawn raincoat, a red-and-white muffler, and an old cap, in case they had to do any foot-tailing. They sheepishly traipsed out of the main entrance, walked down Lord Street, got into the Viva—which looked even more disgusting when compared to Southport traffic—and spluttered off Liverpool-wards.

Then Smithy and I went upstairs to change. Smithy produced out of his attaché case black boots with the big toe separate, black tracksuit bottoms, a cricket-box, and a black top with hood. Black gloves completed the ensemble, and there stood Smithy—your complete ninja. He also took out, checked, and put back into the bag some stun grenades, a gas pistol, an ammonia spray, and a flail.

I was less outrageously dressed, in dark-blue polo neck, dark jeans, and a black leather jacket. I also checked that my police-issue Mauser automatic was working and loaded, and slipped it into the side pocket of my jacket. Finally, I pocketed a wicked-looking spiked knuckleduster that I had taken off an East End gang boss, slipped a standard-issue truncheon up my left sleeve, and issued Smithy and myself pairs of handcuffs—the lightweight wire, self-tightening sort.

Then we too had to run the gauntlet of the dowager-like stares of the front hall as we got into the Capri, checked for a full tank, checked the radio for frequency, and drove slowly into the closing-time traffic.

It was getting light. She woke, happily dreaming of days gone by, when she had lived deliriously on the edge with her Polish boyfriend. The pride seeing him take his Lancaster smoothly into the cold night Scampton air. The relief of seeing the Lanc. return. The lovemaking, giggling quietly in his room, or—dangerously—in the back of the Lanc. "There!" she would say. "I've christened it. It belongs to me. You belong to me." Then, listening to the Polish endearments. Life was good; the Germans were running. This madness would soon cease, and then she and her Pole would go on forever.

Then she awoke to a grey Lancashire dawn. Cold hatred set in. Remembering the Lancaster—her Lancaster—lighting up the dawn sky. Engine blazing, rear turret smashed, fuselage stitched neatly by cannon shells. And as she touched down, the undercarriage collapsing, the flames engulfing the whole plane. Finally, the fire died down so the fire crews could get in, bringing out six charred bodies and one hideously burned radio operator.

Flight Lieutenant Gregson groaned. These days, he existed in a paranoid half-world. He never knew what year he lived in. He was whole days riding round the Ashdown Forest, or fox hunting, dancing with the local Pamelas and Priscillas. But it always turned black. He spent interminable hours trapped in a blazing Lancaster.

His lucid periods were spent trying to disappear into a Teacher's bottle. He ate little. He was sick often. His ribs stuck out. He stank. His daily exercise consisted of the short stagger from bed to lavatory to table. When he ate, it was cold and tinned: cold beans, cold stew, cold rice pudding. The few occasions he ventured outside to collect his pension and buy his few and meagre groceries, he timidly hurried back to his rat's nest as fast as he could. The traffic, the noise, the jostling people frightened and bewildered him.

He didn't know what year it was, but he knew what time of the month it was. He always knew when the hallucinations came around. He knew that like some demonic menstrual cycle, his hallucinations would come today. Always the same. They started with three black-clad Mickey Mouses rough-handling him, and then the nightmare progressed into psychedelic colours, in which the centre was the need to send Morse, voices inexorably chanting five-letter groups.

This climaxed, always, in the nightmare fire, followed by weakness, debility, disorientation. And it got worse every month. Every month, he went that much deeper into the nightmare and took that much longer to come out of it. He had long ago stopped wondering where the monthly crate of Teacher's came from.

Six o'clock came and went. Seven, eight. Gregson opened a new bottle of Teacher's. He curled up in a foetal position on his filthy cot. He closed his eyes tight, in a pathetic and childlike attempt to keep away the bogeymen. Ten o'clock, and he was beginning to relax, doped by the soporific passing of hours and the booze.

Then—*slam!* The door flew back on its hinges, and there were the three Mickey Mouses. George shuddered and crossed himself, rearing back on the bed in terror. Rough hands grabbed him, pushing aside his weak defenceless arms. They grabbed him and threw him face-down on his bed. He moaned at the indignity of his trousers being pulled down, hissed at the jab of a hypodermic in one withered buttock. Then his trousers were dragged painfully and roughly back up, and he was picked up and dragged down the stairs.

A curious old lady peered out of a door. "Boo!" said one Mickey, and the face fled.

George was dragged, unresisting, feet trailing, out to the old green Transit, and thrust in the back. One Mickey got in with him, whilst the other two got into the front, taking off their mouse masks to reveal tough-looking heads. They drove unhurriedly off towards Southport.

At eleven-thirty, the van parked up on the beach behind the Toad Hall Club in Ainsdale. In the back, a Mickey Mouse struggled to hold down a raving Gregson. Whiskey, LSD, and paranoia bubbled in his blood, twitched down his limbs, and ranted out of his mouth. Thrashing, delirious, cursing in English, French, and German, he was proving a real handful to Mickey.

Finally, he was thrust down on the plank seat and quietened with a cigarette. Mickey proceeded to get out of its case the old-fashioned WW2 non-crystal, coil-tuned radio and set it up in front of George.

George slumped on the wooden seat. Great orange and purple starshells burst in his vision. One minute, Mickey Mouse was on fire, then he was an empty skull, then a blue mouse. A Morse key was put in George's hand, sometimes seeming as big as a telegraph pole, sometimes so small he was scared of crushing it. The dials of the radio lit up. It hummed to life, demonically grinning at him.

Mickey clicked the key a few times and watched the needles flick. Then he carefully placed the key near George's paw. At midnight precisely, the wasp sting aerial powered into the night sky. In the van, Mickey began reading—in a clipped, precise voice—five-figure groups. George began to send them as best as he could: NYMOC ABFEV EGIOU STCON ...

Flight Lieutenant Gregson was trapped in a burning bomber; his guts yawed as the dive steepened. His captain was reading groups to him, calmly, as if they were flying smooth and level. *NYMOC ABFEV EGIOU STCON*—the plane lurched as cannon shells thudded into it. The fuselage was burning, bright orange, acid yellow, and pure green. The dive steepened. George's nerve broke ... *SOS ... SOS ... SOS ... EEEE* it screamed as he collapsed over the key.

Mickey cursed and tried to push George free, but George was rigid, locked in a spasm, tight as if the key was screwed down. The plug was immobile under George. Mickey tried to tear out the power-leads, but they wandered out of reach under the seat. He banged on the case, but it was stout mild steel, and all Mickey got was stinging palms. In part-fury, part-panic, he banged on the cab partition.

"Abort, abort!" he screamed. "It's gone wrong! Get out!"

The van lurched into life, gears engaged and van moving even before the whine of the starter had finished. Wheels spinning, it wallowed across the sand, fishtailing as the driver sought traction and acceleration on the wet sand. Then there was a *bang!* as the van stopped dead.

Ted, Ken, and Alan drove fairly briskly into Liverpool, despite the fag-end of the nightlife traffic. At the police HQ, they split and drew matches for the Viva. Ted was the unlucky one: He won. Ken and Alan gratefully and happily accepted a D-reg 1800 and a new Capri. After gleefully and childishly playing with the walkie-talkies, they set out in convoy for Kowalski's pad.

As they approached Liverpool 8, the bantering mood solidified, and they became professional and taut. The cars spaced out, putting other vehicles between them. It was agreed at police HQ that they should park out of sight of Kowalski's terraced house and let the regular CID watchers give them the go-ahead. These were situated on the top floor of the old warehouse, where they had full view of both the front and rear of Kowalski's.

They parked in separate streets and settled down, walkie-talkies on *receive*, to await the one word, "Amphora", which meant Kowalski was moving. Ted read the *Liverpool Echo* he had thoughtfully provided for himself. Ken did a crossword. Alan browsed through his one-shilling copy of Butler's *Erewhon*.

Then, at 7 o'clock, came the word "Amphora"—followed by "Wheels up, oncer," which meant he was driving, going north, alone. The three cars unobtrusively slotted in behind Kowalski, but all were glad when he reached the dock road and the thicker traffic. From there, the three cars played ducks and drakes, keeping whenever possible two cars between the lead and Kowalski. Kowalski turned up Sandhills Lane and threaded his way to the A59.

Me and Smithy cruised up and down Lord Street, then, for a change, up and down the front. Then vice versa. Once, we even ventured along the sea-wall road, but only once; we needed to be near the centre of the action. I willed myself to drive smoothly and carefully, not jerkily, despite the tension building up in my limbs and the adrenalin flowing as midnight approached.

Smithy sat, a spindly electronic spider, two radios and a map-table having been very quickly cobbled into the front passenger space. One radio was a police transceiver tuned into the D/F vans, the other a powerful Racal receiver tuned to Matey's frequency. Down at Mugglesby, Paul was backup operator on Matey's frequ, with two more operators searching the frequencies in the somewhat vain hope that if Matey changed his frequ, they could find him. A similar search was being made at Southport police HQ. There were also backup D/F operations at Mugglesby, up the Liverpool post-office tower, and at the Lancashire police HQ in Hutton. Whilst these were of necessity not as pinpoint-accurate as our three vans, they were belt-and-braces if something went wrong—or if the bogeymen moved out of the area.

Meanwhile, as I drove, because I couldn't bear just to park and do nothing, I could feel the large key in my back tightening my spring. But Smithy went about his tasks exuding calmness. He laid out the large-scale map on the impromptu table. He checked that the receiver was receiving. He called up Mugglesby and the six D/F vans in turn, and then he sat back in his comatose prayer-position. This irritated me.

"Why the blazes do you have to be so calm?" I asked.

Smithy opened one eye. "Eh? Oh, contemplative prayer."

"Yeah, but how do you square that?"

"It's difficult, but it's down—you saw the effect on me in Southport after Brody was murdered—but it's down, at least in my mind, to original sin, mine and everybody else's. When my wife and little child were killed, I could have assassinated that clumsy driver, very slowly and very painfully. And I could have done the same to everyone on a charge of careless driving, dangerous driving, or drunk in charge. I spent months wanting to meet that idiot down a dark alley. Forgiving that tanker-driver was the hardest thing I've ever had to do. It nearly broke me. Do you see now why I had to go to Whitby? Yet there, I found peace."

Appalled at the chasm my pre-action hype had caused, I muttered "urgh" and drove on.

The hype got more and more hyped, the silence got tenser and tenser, as I drove one-handed and checked and rechecked the Mauser. The dashboard clock metronomed thin slices of eternity towards midnight. Smithy began to show tension in his hooded gaze, in the stillness of every line of his body, and in his tuneless half-hiss, half-whistle.

Fifteen seconds later came the Morse: *NYMOC ABFEV EGIOU STCON* ... then madness! *SOS SOS SOS* degenerating into a scream of carrier wave.

Quickly, Smithy called the three vans in turn, swiftly drawing in the D/F-lines as they were given.

"Right, Bill, head out on the Liverpool road!"

I screamed the Capri round in a handbrake turn and powered off down Lord Street. Weaving in and out of traffic, missing the late-night home-dawdlers by a coat-of paint thickness, boring down the centre line at speeds well over the legal or safe limit, listening to Smithy's direction, I drove with all the fired-up skill that Hendon Police Driving School and a quart of adrenaline could impart. Smithy, meanwhile, kept up a monotone of instructions.

"Looks like at or near, far as I can tell, a club called Toad Hall. There's a lot of beach there. They could easily get away." On Smithy's instructions, I turned onto the coast road, screaming along, 75, 80, 85, past the courting couples and adulterers, towards Toad Hall.

Meanwhile, Ken, Ted, and Alan had played ducks-and-drakes with Kowalski all the way to Preston. The only worry occurred at the County Road traffic lights in Ormskirk, when, through sheer carelessness, they found themselves in line astern behind the green Transit. However, Ken and Ted peeled off left and right, Ken going down Southport Road, Grimshaw Lane, and Yew Tree Road, regaining the main road at the Burscough Street junction. Alan gunned the Nova past the van, following from in front till past Burscough, when he allowed the van to retake him.

The convoy straggled into Preston, the Transit leading them through the backstreets, finally stopping outside a rundown old Victorian large terrace, obviously flats. Ken and Alan, in the new cars, continued. Alan drove on, turned round, and pulled up down the road. Ted in the Viva—most fitting in that street—did a three-point turn and parked, ready to go.

"They've gone into flat three, no. 127, all three," he reported.

Minutes passed. Then, "Hang on! There's four of them coming out, our original three in Mickey Mouse masks, dark shirts, and trousers, almost carrying an old guy. Poor old sod. Looks bewildered." Pause while Ted took some low-light shots with infrared telephoto.

Ken ostentatiously pulled up outside another block of flats and disappeared into the doorway. Alan drove past and parked in a side road, raincoat on, Ted's paper under his arm. This was not the sort of street a man could loiter insignificantly in, but thankfully, there was a fish-and-chip shop open, with a queue. Alan joined the queue and had just been served when he saw four people emerge—one being almost carried out to the van. Kowalski and the two other large-shouldered plug-uglies dumped the fourth person none too gently in the back.

As the van lumbered towards the main road, Alan spoke into his walkie-talkie: "Green Ford van, same one, B-reg, coming towards you, Ken."

"Roger," Ken answered, starting the motor.

Ted came round the corner, door open. Alan jumped in and jumped out at his car, still clutching his fish and chips, as Ted turned purposefully northward to join the chase.

"They're getting into the van. Taken their masks off. They're moving. Whoever's nearest, pick them up at the corner. Over—now out."

Ken in the 1800 picked up the Transit and followed it out of Preston. By now it was dark, and it's a lot easier and safer shadowing behind dipped headlights. The van loitered through Croston, picked up Southport Road, and kept to a decorous forty that was easy to shadow. Passing through Southport, they took the coast road, turning right at Toad Hall Island and driving openly and innocuously on the beach.

Alan, who was then immediately behind, drove straight on to allay any suspicions, then turned an awkward three-pointer and returned to park in the Toad Hall car park. Meanwhile, Ted and Ken separately drove onto the sand, two midnight cowboys. Ted stopped a hundred yards short of the van, whilst Ken drove a hundred yards past it. By now, both Ted and Ken had the van in sight through powerful night glasses, whilst Alan, in touch by radio, waited as backup—a trapdoor spider.

11.59. The giant wasp sting of an aerial emerged silently from the van. They waited, hoping the van was transmitting, hoping the D/F vans were receiving, hoping that Smithy was acting. Uneasily, separately, all three assembled their SMGs, slipped knives into waistbands, and blacked-up, quickly and efficiently.

Then, suddenly, action. The van started—motor whirring frantically, van moving, fishtailing, slipping sideways as much as forwards. A second's indecision. What to do? Act? Or follow? Then "Go!" yelled Ted and hurled the Viva forward. It met the Transit with a crunching mechanical embrace, the Transit mounting the Viva. The front window of the Transit shattered; a black machine-gun snout sniffed the air, then burped flame at the Viva.

Ted the fit, Ted the efficient, Ted above all the married, died in a hail of foreign bullets.

Ken hurled himself at the rear door of the Transit. The back door cautiously opened then slammed shut as Ken's Uzi spat deterrent. Alan screamed round the corner, lightless, and rolled clear even before the car had stopped moving. Hate spat from the windscreen, followed by the gruff boom of a repeat-action shotgun. Glass tinkled from the back window, and a submachine gun tested the scent for Ken—invisible but very vulnerable, alone on the open sand.

Smithy and I roared towards the action, pulling on black balaclavas. Smithy urgently calling in backup of SPG as we went. As we sped towards the scene, we could see and hear a battle up ahead. We screamed onto the sand, both doors open while the Capri was still rolling. We rolled clear. I rose on one knee with pistol cocked and ready, while Smithy, ghost silent, dematerialised and rematerialised by my side a moment later. I shot out of my skin and nearly shot him.

"Alan reporting. Ted's down. Ken's pinned on the sand. Four of them in. Distract them for me." And Smithy was gone.

I loosed two shots in quick succession—*blam, blam!*—then rolled away as the shotgun threw a handful of lethal hail to patter on the sand that I had pressed. I loosed two more shots, then rolled back. Once more, the gruff shotgun's voice and innocuous-sounding pattering.

Then all hell let loose: a thunderflash under the van, a smoke bomb through the shattered front window, stun grenades on the van's tin sides, and a screaming flare to light the scene in harsh primary colour. I jumped to my feet as the back door opened, helping out the escaping thug. He rolled onto the sand, reflex-kicking me in the gut as he did so. Though winded, I jumped on him with both knees, fingers feeling for the soft under-jaw and eyes. In turn, he loosed another kick. Thankfully, I dodged, and only got a numbed thigh.

We rolled around feeling for the advantage, gouging, kicking, butting in a frenzy of vicious mutual attack. Finally, he made a mistake. In attempting to scissors my head, he left his groin vulnerable. A stiff finger poke in the genitals left him sobbing helplessly on the sand, and before you could say "castration," I had the cuffs on him, Ken rushed in, clobbered him with the SMG butt, and then moved to cover the back doors again.

I hauled myself onto my feet, puffing like a grampus's grandad, and leapt round the front.

One guy was lying face down on the sand, with Alan standing on him, Uzi resting on neck. But in the dimming glare of the flare, I saw Smithy in silent, deadly struggle with Kowalski. Kowalski—muscled, brutal, bull-like—rushed Smithy, bellowing and trying to smother him with brute strength. Smithy was a mere shadow out of which a nunchaku cracked, producing howls of rage and pain from Kowalski. Then an ankle-high flail-sweep brought Kowalski to his knees, and before he could rise, the fail thwacked him in the back of the neck, and he fell, a matadored bull on the wet sand.

I rushed in and handcuffed him, and we dragged the three bodies together, using the spare cuffs to fasten their ankles tight. Then we silently reinforced Ken—Alan and I at the front window, Ken and Smithy at the back door. From inside came a peculiar sobbing wail.

Ken reached gingerly for the door handle and threw it aside. Alan flicked in a stun grenade and a smoke bomb, then fell flat. After the noise, nothing happened. Ken continued to cover the door as Smithy cautiously started the 1800, pulled up behind the van, and got out, reaching back in to switch on the headlights. In the far corner was a barely human shape, gibbering and stammering with its arm shielding its eyes, flat blind panic in the remnant of a face.

Just then, late as always, two vanloads of SPG screamed up and surrounded us with lights, noise, and guns. Smithy stood up, stretched, and sighed.

7

THE NEXT FEW HOURS WERE CHAOS. BECAUSE THE VAN HAD NOT finished its transmission, we were not too sure of what to expect. We worked it down to Bedfordshire, but the jumbled letter groups, probably inaccurate, definitely shaky, were not of any real use to us. Next day, when a British Midland 737 ran out of runway at Luton Airport following an explosion in the left-hand engine and slid expensively along the concrete on its nose, to the embarrassment of BM but without loss of life, we sighed with relief and got on with the investigation.

The following day, Smithy insisted we go down to Hereford to visit Ted's wife and children. That was awful! The two SAS lads and Alan's wife surrounded her with silent, heartfelt sympathy. Ted's wife was a public-school blond, rapidly disappearing national characteristic of stiff upper lip very much in evidence, but very fragile, red-eyed, and beyond misery. The children, two girls and a boy, stared at us in wide-eyed horror, bewildered, proud of their dad, resentful of two strangers, and grieving as only a child can. I sat there awkward and tongue-tied, while Smithy talked and listened.

And how he talked! I expected religious claptrap, somehow, of the *dulce et decorum est* variety, but no. Smithy explained, boldly, how Ted had died, alone, in a crushed, burnt-out old banger, killed by a Sten machine gun—World War II standard issue, obsolete but no less a killer for being outdated. Neither did he utter bilge like how Ted hadn't died in vain. With Smithy's theology of human wickedness but human preciousness, every death this side of threescore and ten was a waste. Smithy stated this boldly, with a sort of reassurance: "Never be afraid to grieve. Never let anyone tell you it's not that bad. It is. It's every bit that bad. And if I can help in any way whatsoever, please ring me at this number. And don't think I'm not right in there. I lost my wife and daughter three years ago. I still miss them."

And without further ado, he shook hands—a stilted old-fashioned gesture—with Ted's widow, put his arms around Ted's kids, and after a brief hug, left swiftly and completely, with me following in his wake, leaving the SAS to grieve their own.

We had a silent, awkward, grief-stricken drive back up M5, M6, M62, then Smithy dropped off at Karen's and I drove back, silent and thoughtful, to Southport.

Meanwhile, the old mad guy had been manhandled into an ambulance and put under guard in Southport Hospital.

Ted was due to be buried with full military honours at Hereford, and all his children wanted to keep was his sand-coloured beret and winged dagger badge.

Smithy and Karen insisted on taking care of the old lunatic we'd found in the van. They insisted on taking him down to a drugs clinic run by a church in Bristol that would dry him out and bring him down from the lampshades. Smithy and Karen took him down there personally, a two-day journey, just time for me to bring Nessie up from London for a much needed R&R, scandalising the Scarisbrick clientele once more.

This was after Karen had insisted on taking the old guy home, showering him, feeding him, and kitting him out in her dad's second best. Kindness, food, and the warmth of the White family brought him to the point where he could remember that his name was George Gregson, that he was an ex-flight lieutenant, and that he was 48 years old. He told us his disfigured face had been the result of a WWII Lancaster crash. But little else could he remember, other than the paranoid nightmare of being back in his burning Lanc. with three mice, trying desperately to radio someone.

Despite these brief periods of lucidity, he wasn't an easy passenger. Blood samples had revealed LSD mixing with the blood in his alcohol stream. So the journey down must have been a nightmare; a raving alky and acid head mixing with Smithy's demonic driving would, I thought, have turned Karen white overnight, but when they turned up on the third day back at the Scarisbrick, she was triumphantly the Masai princess as ever. And the sparkle of the seven-diamond cluster on her left hand caused a faraway gleam in Nessie's eyes, with periods of cerebrating silence.

Then it was back to work, because we hadn't succeeded in achieving much—not much at all. Catalogue: one dead colleague, three arrested heavies, one old drunk on detox. One smashed-up van and one radio that Noah must have got his weather reports on. And one dead end. No idea of who the paymasters were, who the organisation was, or where to go from here. We were in a forked stick. Sure, we had broken up the communications department of a nasty terrorist bunch—vicious but small-time—but we still had no idea of why they were doing it or if they had the ability to continue it.

We kicked ideas round endlessly. "Was it political?" I pondered. "Was it criminal? It's a cold, callous little clique we're dealing with. The monthly disregard for life proved that—not to mention the swift dispatch of J. Brady and the uncaring, systematic torture, degradation, and drugging of the old flight lieutenant. But with what in mind? And what of those to whom the messages were sent? Where were they? *Who* were they? What will replace the green Transit?"

"That above all," Smithy conjectured. "What will replace the green Transit? The possibilities are endless—CB, radio, telephone, the dead-letter box loved by spies everywhere ... all virtually untraceable. And the incidents will probably go on, and on, until finally we get a break and the whole mess is stopped. Leaving how many dead? How much money lost? How much unrest? How much damage? Grief? Unnecessary pain? And why?"

We retreated back to Mugglesby, five days a week. Weekends, Smithy panzered his way across country in the Viva to Liverpool and Karen's. I caught a fast smooth Deltic from Lincoln to London and Nessie. Ken and Alan had returned to Hereford.

8

THE TIME BACK AT MUGGLESBY WAS ODD. WE SAT IN OUR HIDEY-HOLE. We shuffled little cards and big maps. As time passed and our whiz-kid image faded, the Mugglesby CO got less and less accommodating and more and more irritable. Watch commanders got more and more unhelpful.

Then Smithy and I were ordered to Whitehall and then ordered—*ordered,* mark you!—to produce results. Which was being duffed-up with a feather for Smithy. He was the unflappable Don Quixote. He was civvy. He was untouchable. Me, I had a pension to think about.

Our committee consisted of one Air-rank from the RAF, one very senior copper, one high-grade from GCHQ, and one Whitehall Warrior. The Heavy Mob were gathered round the conference table, RAF-type, dressed in soft barathea uniforms with chestfuls of medals, probably gained for waiting in NAAFI queues. The two civvies were dressed in expensive lounge suits. *What an honour,* I sardonically said to myself.

Smithy appeared in the conference room with a clipboard, very intelligent-looking, dressed in sand-coloured slacks, big-collar shirt, and a scarf round his neck—his *I'm an intellectual* persona. I put on my rarely worn Chief Super's uniform and medals, mine gained the hard way.

Each attendee questioned us closely, some with parade-ground barks, some in quiet-and-deadly mode, and the one from the Home Office so sweetly, slimily reasonable he must have left a trail when he walked. The interrogation went on and on, and round and round, same old questions, same old answers. I was beginning to wonder if a pension was worth it.

Then Smithy paused. He blinked. He cleared his throat and started in.

"Why are we here?" he mildly asked. "Why the interrogation? Do you want this job done? Don't you read our daily reports?" He regarded this very senior cadre with power over life, death, and pensions, and said, "If so, stop all this waste of time and effort in browbeating Bill and me, and let us get on with it! If you don't, I will go back to Whitby, and you can sort your own mess out. After all, this was your idea."

He added, "There is one lead open, and that's the Three Graces we have captured. But we must have a free hand. Bill?"

"Gentlemen," I began, "this is the way it seems to me. Firstly, the prisoners. I recommend we grill two and let one go. With a steady grilling, we may get some leads. Not very likely—it's bound to be worked on the closed-cell system—but we may get a name, a drop-off point, a clue.

"Likewise, if we let Kowalski go, he must, sooner or later, lead us to the next step on the staircase. He is the only Pole; the others are low-grade British hooligans, all brawn and no brain, ten a penny. Kowalski's got both, so he must be team leader and contact point. We can get him sprung believably."

At this point, I handed over to Smithy, who said, "Then communications. This is a fine-tuned long-distance clumsy net. It won't be easy to change. If they intend to continue it, logically it may continue this way. And it has to receive its orders from someone. And why a radio net? Most probably because ordinary phone lines couldn't so easily or quite so clandestinely be used. But in emergency, phones could be used. Or even by post or that good old spy standby, the dead-letter drop. The radio presupposes out-of-country." Nod in the direction of GCHQ. "Which means someone knows that all international calls can be monitored. Which means incoming intelligence will be by radio as well. To someone known to us. Because it also presupposes the possibility of phone taps."

They were agog. What a team we made! All the empire-building brass, sitting there, mouths open, listening to us build card-houses!

"So you have a choice, gentlemen," Smithy continued. "If you want to close this operation down, then do so! But remember consequences. If you allow us to continue in this fashion and continue to back us, then we *may*—I stress *may*, gentlemen—we *may* be able to dig the roots out. Or we may not. They may go away. Or invent a new annoyance. It's fairly low-grade, after all."

"So," grumbled the bespectacled PUS from the Home Office, also called Smith, "why, if it's low-grade, de we need expensively to retain you and Superintendent Watson, Mr Smith, and why the SAS, the police vans, and all the other costly gewgaws you've inflicted on us?"

As he spoke, I saw the trap yawn. Other-Smith didn't. He walked right in. And as Smithy's favourite light reading says, "Great was the fall thereof."

No gleam of satisfied killer instinct was allowed out of Smithy's eyes, but I knew he had picked his mark and lured his fly into his parlour. The irritation manifest on the faces round the table let me gather that Other-Smith was Not Popular, and his downfall would be a whole headdress of feathers in our caps.

Smithy leaned forward courteously. "Because," he said in an ultra-reasonable voice (think tutor with a keen but backward student), "firstly, though low-grade, it has proved costly in lives, in danger, in nuisance to the rescue services, and in money. I have some breakdowns on figures." Smithy riffled his clipboard pseudo-clumsily, beamed, and handed everyone a neatly typed sheet. The crafty old fleabag! And now I knew the reason for some of the distracted silences and cabbalistic mutterings of late.

"Secondly," he continued when the rhubarb and paper rustling had died down, "it may be just a distraction, while something much nastier and more clandestine goes on underneath. You know, if you want someone who's streetwise followed, you stick a fat man in a check cap on his tail, and a little grey ferret on the fat man's tail. The mark recognises the tail, shakes him, and goes off congratulating himself, with the little grey ferret glued to his hindquarters. This monthly mayhem *may*—again I stress *may*—be of this order. If we let it go, we may be storing up worse trouble. If we keep at it, *we* may be distraction to *them*, and digging at it may uncover any plan B."

Smithy paused to look around the room, then continued.

"Thirdly, this is the moral issue. We are all professionally committed to keeping the peace and the continuation of our culture and our chosen way of life, throughout this society and regardless of fear or favour. Any less is failure to do our jobs."

Smithy leaned imperceptibly forwards, skewered each in turn with a cool eye, and awaited the results. Nods from Copper, RAF type and GCHQ, Pause, then reluctant grumbled acquiescence from Other-Smith.

"What we propose ..."

The crafty old hoodlum! He'd won them lock, stock, and barrel: four professional cynics accepting sugar lumps from a wild moorland recluse! After all, they had pensions to think about too. Grumbling, untrusting, our Beloved Führers turned us loose to dig, to think, to work, and to stop monthly chaos—but keep the cost down.

Back at Mugglesby, we called a council of war. The next disaster date, if we could rely on it, was getting closer. After the go-ahead from the joint committee, the Mugglesby CO warmed up and eagered up tremendously, and we went back to plotting. I was given the oversight of Kowalski's interrogation, and Ken and Alan were brought back to do some SAS nastiness on the other two terrorists.

Up in Liverpool's Walton Jail, Kowalski proved to be a hard case, mentally and physically. He was strong, tough, and streetwise, and that fairly rare bird: a bully who wasn't a coward. He had fought the Germans in the Warsaw ghetto; he had fought the Russians in the uprising; and he had run a criminal black-market gang in post-war Warsaw. He knew the legal ropes and seemed unhassled when I didn't allow him his phone call. In fact, he was unhassled whatever I did or said. He sat there like a granite Polish Buddha, accepting cigarettes, coffee, and meals without thanks, only speaking to say: "I want a lawyer."

The only time his granite persona cracked was when I said to him, "You don't half fancy yourself, Kowalski, don't you! Sat there like a poor girl's Charles Bronson."

His face lit up; he beamed. "Oh, do you really t'ink so? T'ank you," he said and sat there for the next five minutes silently beaming instead of silently scowling.

By the third day of illegal detainment, I was getting sick of Kowalski, all of the screws in Walton Jail were getting sick of Kowalski, I suspect even Kowalski was getting sick of Kowalski. And the time for the next disaster was getting nearer—an explosive menstrual cycle.

Easy, Bill, I told myself, *it's you who've got PMT.* I smiled wryly at myself, caught Kowalski looking, and snarled at him.

Just then, a ruction manifested itself in the corridor outside. The door flew back, and into the room, propelling some poor little police cadet ahead of him, flew a vision of legal loveliness.

For there, agitated and clucking furiously, stood Smithy, clad in too-short, too-wide-striped trousers and dusty old black jacket, bent spectacles flying somewhere near his nose, hair awry ... I couldn't believe it! Before my gob had time to open too wide or my jaw got much past my knees, Smithy rushed forward, saying—or gasping—"Mr Ko-wal-sky, I have been retained by the court as your legal representative. *Three days!* This case must be dismissed! It's, it's, it's ... *illegal!*"

He turned on me. "Superintendent," he boomed. He paused, drew himself up, opened his briefcase, and, like the Great Mystico producing rabbits, produced paper after paper.

"*This*, Superintendent," slamming it down, "is a writ of habeas corpus. *This*" (smack on the table) "is a move for Mr Kowalski's release, and *this* is to serve *you* for wrongful arrest!"

Entering into the spirit, I blustered, I bullied, I wheedled, I cajoled, I stood on regulations, I stood on my dignity, but at last I allowed the verbal kung fu to triumph and got Kowalski sprung.

As soon as the last paper was signed, Kowalski disappeared out of that place like a Polish badger with its bum on fire, whilst Smithy and I clutched each other and rocked and grimaced in silent merriment like a couple of schoolkids.

When the hysterics had passed, Smithy said coolly, "Kowalski's got four of the best Liverpool fuzz on his tail; the other two morons have been interrogated and charged. All we know is they were recruited by Kowalski on a retainer basis, both have got form going back to mugging their midwives, and with any sort of justice should get at least ten, preferably on the Moor. In the meantime, we're trying to troll the records of police, GCHQ, MI5&6, SIS ... oh, anyone and everyone to bring up anyone with a profile of possible security risks, street-and-legal-wise, likely knows South-West Lancs, but definitely knows England; no offshore, Scottish, or Irish disasters so far; knows radio, especially old time valve-sets. That should be only slightly more difficult than looking for a needle in a Dutch barn full of hay."

Smithy announced, as we were going to Liverpool, that he was off to Karen's for tea, did I want to come? Being at a loose end, and rather liking the black-and-white Whites, as well as being a great admirer of young Karen, I agreed. After tea, Smithy and Karen said they were off out.

"Where to?" I asked. "Which sauve, elegant boîte-de-nuit are you gracing tonight?"

I got the answer I had expected: a prayer meeting. How, I wondered aloud once more, could Smithy reconcile mayhem, baddie-conning, and high-powered security stuff with, of all things, a prayer meeting?

"You've got it back-to-front," Karen told me. "This lot is a chimera; a nothing. In a hundred years, no one will remember you, me, Ted the SAS man, or this mucky little backstreet war, but God is eternal."

"Does that include dusty old church halls and old biddies in hats?" I asked.

Smithy jumped in with an offer of "come and see how wrong you are," but I declined and, excusing myself hurriedly but graciously, shot back to Southport for a pint.

Later, we drove back to Mugglesby. The next day found Smithy and me down to nitpicking. Smithy fell back into his old routine of wearing out his knees by his bed, jogging round the camp, then fiddling with bits of paper in the section, but with a new routine. He constantly rang Karen and seemed to write a book to her every day.

But that very week, something broke. Perhaps my interrogation techniques are better than I thought, or Smithy's legal persona convinced Kowalski of how soppy us British were, because he committed the cardinal sin of going straight back to his flat and using his own telephone. We'd been there before him, and the phone was bugged. He didn't stop to check. So when he rang up the Bulgarian Embassy, we had a nice clear tape to applaud.

It would be wrong to say Kowalski had panicked—Mount Fujiyama would have panicked first—but certainly he was rattled. The transcript of the tape showed him urgently calling, in Polish, to be taken out of the country. There was a bit of an argument, and then an agreement that a Bulgarian attaché would meet him in Liverpool. Kowalski demanded money and a false passport, and promised silence. His masters slammed down the phone with less grace and gratitude than their little boy merited.

But 6.30 in the buffet at Skelhorne Street bus station, they said, and 6.30 at Skelhorne Street it would be. With us there to applaud.

So, back to Liverpool—the Capri should get there on its own by now—to meet Mr Kowalski and his boss.

9

SIX-TWENTY-FIVE FOUND US LURKING AROUND SKELHORNE STREET. IN front of us paced the Neanderthal Kowalski. I lurked behind a hastily erected GPO telephone tent, legs halfway down a manhole cover, Pentax with zoom lens at the ready. I was well hidden in woolly hat and donkey jacket, for Kowalski had spent a lot of time with me lately.

Smithy lounged openly, green combat jacket, Rasta wig, rucksack, and blackface—so perfectly camouflaged that he had actually asked Kowalski for a light and received it. One day his quirky sense of humour would get him into real trouble. Across the way, three plain-clothes Liverpool coppers lounged behind their *Daily Mirrors*.

The Liver Birds had just crowed 6.32 when a small dark-clad Mr Average, complete with attaché case and rolled brolly, paddled up to Kowalski and spoke briefly to him. They had unhurriedly moved off, pushing through the crowd, when something spooked them. Perhaps it was one of the Plods moving a bit hastily, but Mr Average slapped Kowalski and said, "Go!" They began running out of the bus station. The three coppers ran after them. Smithy stepped to intercept them.

Mr Average's brolly licked out, a striking metal snake, and Smithy fell, writhing, face contorted, foaming at the mouth. Kowalski and Average leapt into a taxi, which did an illegal U-turn, caromed off the side of a bus, and disappeared into the rush-hour traffic outside St George's Hall.

I turned back to the bus station and pushed through the gawping crowds. Smithy was quiet now, lying still, pale, and deathly sweaty on the pavement. The ambulance took an eternity to arrive but finally got here, ingested the red-blanket cocoon into its gape, and two-toned its way to the Royal Infirmary.

I broke out the Capri and scorched up London Road. I waited to see Smithy into intensive care, the drips attached and the oxygen mask in place, ECG bleeping away, monotonously slicing Smithy's life into forty-per-minute strips, and then I left with heavy heart to tell Karen.

I drove slowly, putting off the time I would see Karen, but at last I sat down face-to-face and blurted out, "Karen, John's hurt. Desperately. Poisoned. We don't know what with yet. I'm sorry."

Karen went very still. Then her head came up. Suddenly, she was the real Masai princess. She stood up, very slowly, very controlled. "Bill, you must take me there—now!"

We stayed with Smithy until told to go home by a sympathetic but tired and harassed doctor. All the tests were being done. Smithy was stable but still on a ventilator, and much of his body was paralysed. I drove Karen home. She, still very much under the obvious control, insisted I stay. Then she retired, still under iron-gutted control. It wasn't until three hours later that I woke on the settee to the sound of Karen's heavy, heartbroken sobbing: "O God, O Lord God, don't let him die, not now. Please no." The Iron Maiden had finally cracked.

Three days passed. Three days in which the taxi was found and identified—stolen in Garston the night of the attack. Three days in which the poison was identified—a form of artificially manufactured curare not unknown on the tips of Bulgarian brollies in the last few years. Three days in which Smithy lay like a corpse, kept alive only by a thin thread of technology. Three days in which Karen walked publicly like a tight-lipped black ghost and wept and prayed in private.

Then, after three days, a phone call from the hospital: come quickly, signs of life in Smithy, signs of hope.

We sat, Karen, Karen's mum and dad, and I round Smithy's bed. He didn't seem much changed, just more restless. But his heart had speeded up and strengthened, and his breathing—still on the ventilator—stabilised. Then his eyelids fluttered and opened, and he came round, typically Smithy, quoting, "The Lord is my shepherd, I shall not want, He makes me lie down in green pastures …"

He opened his eyes with a start, looked up, smiled, and said, "Hello, you lot. I'm hungry ..."

The grey Mersey dawn arose across the grey Mersey water. The day awoke sluggishly: cold, drizzly, and damp. Cats prowled miserably. Rats scuttled dispiritedly. Milkmen shuffled and cursed. Beat-coppers sniffed, blew on fingers, and looked at watches.

And a corpse wallowed in the grey Mersey tide.

10

Once Smithy came round, he got better hand overfist. He ate ravenously and within a week was discharged and beginning to make efforts to conquer the long slope back to fitness. He was, of course, ensconced in the White's spare room, whilst, to be nearer to Smithy for conferences, liaison, etc. (i.e. to be a gopher), I moved into a small, fairly comfortable hotel in Liverpool.

I also managed to get Ken and Alan back from Hereford. We would need them. Kowalski was a wild animal: crafty, intelligent, and at home in his environment, and whilst our Bulgarian friend must be fairly efficient to down Smithy, despite his Mr Average appearance, Kowalski had taken him out, poison-brolly and all.

Smithy and I coordinated a new search spearheaded by our team of experienced operators at Mugglesby. Unfortunately, if there was a transmission, we missed it.

That is, until we read of a train disaster in the Sheffield suburbs. Three people were killed and twenty-four injured when an electric train ran into two forty-gallon drums filled with concrete, painted black and placed on a busy line. Matey's way of telling us he's still in business, a thumbing of the nose at whoever snatched Gregson—namely us!

Now I too was taking it personally. I was getting angry, longing to grasp the throat of whoever had masterminded this plot and squeeze until the last cruel little spark in the last sadistic brain cell was snuffed out. I caught myself. I mustn't let emotion come into it. Once it got personal, I knew my mind would cloud and my physical fighting skills boil over. Then ... *what the heck*, I shrugged.

The same night, I went out and got riotously drunk. I was put to bed by a concerned Ken and Alan, who did a good job of stopping me fighting anybody and everybody, or annoying anything in skirts, and shutting me up from roaring out obscene songs.

I woke next morning ... sort of. Classic hangover; little gnomes with picks and shovels in a skull segmented like a mouldy orange, gut churning like a washing machine on fast spin, and eyeballs working, sort of, independent of each other and of me. Black mood and spaghetti legs.

The phone added its frenzied ear-sawing to the pain centres. "Ullo," I croaked at it.

Smithy's every word went booming and roaring in hobnails round my skull: "Get over here fast, Bill, please, things are moving again."

I crawled out of bed, shuddering as I put my feet down on the chilly flooring, each foot feeling like a pumpkin with nerve endings. Gritting my teeth, I eventually managed to catch them and fit manic-cobra socks onto their thirty toes, despite a surge of bile in the throat and an extra Kango hammer in the head. Eventually, I got quasi-autonomous legs into openly rebellious jeans, pulled on a clammy denim jacket, downed three Alka-Seltzers, and staggered out to look for a taxi to the bus stop. The diesel stink and lurching of the bus did nothing for the head or the bilious gut, but I eventually managed the journey without throwing. up.

I was feeling slightly less crepuscular when I eventually got to the Whites', but I was not really up to Smithy, still delicate but in high-powered mode. He looked pale and a bit limp, but the laser points were back in the eyes, and behind the weariness was the old familiar tautness.

"Bad news," he said in place of greeting. "Our old friend, the Bulgarian who stabbed me, has turned up dead! In the Mersey. Neck broken, manually. No sign of the brolly, no ID, and disowned by the Bulgarian Embassy."

"Kowalski," I growled.

"Exactly," Smithy replied.

"So we've got to get to him before the Bulgarians do," I mused. "They obviously wanted to stitch up Kowalski's loose end, and he's proved even nastier than we thought."

"So we put out a red alert for him. Surely a large, foreign-sounding oaf can't stay hidden too long."

"But that applies to the Bulgarians as well," I thought out loud.

"Precisely," Smithy said. "So we think, then we move. Now then, does he lie low in Liverpool, does he hide in a Polish community somewhere, or does he go … oh, somewhere else, London or another city?"

"Unlikely to go for another Polish community," I said. "The Poles are fairly honest, open, and integrated—not really a ghetto mentality. He'd show up too easily. So he's local or fled. He certainly can't escape through any of the obvious ports or airports—he's too big and odd-looking to disguise himself. So we look local, and we poke into his background."

"Right, so we look locally, we continue to bug his flat, we get the fuzz to put the word out to the informers, and we pry around that club in Liverpool 8. And we need Ken and Alan to keep sniffing round the other lowlife pubs and clubs."

I briefed Ken and Alan about what had happened: Smithy nearly being murdered by a Bulgarian suspected of being a hit man from Service 7, the assassination wing of Bulgarian State Security, who had now been found floating in the Mersey with a broken neck. "Guess who?" I asked. "So be very careful. I know you guys are genuine hard cases, but this guy is really not nice to tangle with."

Smithy continued, "We're also still turning over possible moles to head this lot up. Five have managed to rake up several. But we should be able to cut that lot down. Remember the parameters: knows round here well, knows old radios, known security risk. Can we add anything else?"

"All the time, Eastern Europe crops up," I answered. "Kowalski, the Bulgarian, his embassy, the known use of poisoned umbrella tips—all point to the Bear's cubs."

"Yes, well-thought Bill, plus the very complicated, old-fashioned, slow means of communication; surely the only reason for such an inefficient system would be to cut out someone who could otherwise be an obvious candidate. And it's got to be freelance or maybe sponsored. Any government clandestines are much too efficient and well-equipped. So we look very carefully indeed at any likely lads that the computers throw at us. We can leave most of the search for Kowalski to the Thin Blue Line. But we must personally scrutinise the computer lists and paper trails."

So back we traipse across the Snake Pass to Mugglesby. And there we sit and bang our brains out, boring ourselves silly and making our eyes bug, playing computer games and card-shuffling with suspects: trade union officials, teachers, journalists, Labour and Conservative Party stalwarts,

Oxford dons, and policemen who were suspected of hard-line Marxist activities. Or, indeed, hard-line Nazi sympathisers. Plus, of course, any Mugglesby operators on the take—thinking of the chief tech busted the year before coming out of the Russian embassy with eight hundred quid in his pocket. Most could be easily eliminated; the very special skills needed, the geographical·knowledge, plus the force of personality to get the Kowalski team on the road were not easily forthcoming or readily available to every Tom, Dick, or Vanya.

A month passed. On D-day, we had a choice: a fire in a barracks, a major crash on the M1 when a French juggernaut's steering inexplicably failed and it crossed over into the path of twelve cars and a bus, or an armed robbery in Wakefield. Not a trace of any R/T transmission on any frequ. So, were we paranoid, or was it Matey still up and about?

And the boredom went on. Check and double-check. Keep R/T watch for the elusive mini-needle of a thirty-second burst of Morse in the infinite haystack of the airwaves, in case the timing had changed.

So it continued. Eight hours gut-crushing, boring, eye-bugging work; work out in the camp gym; pint in the NAAFI or the locals; Smithy jogging and praying; alternate weekends off, me down in the Smoke, Smithy up in the Pool. We did, of course, keep an electronic and visual watch on the Bulgarian Embassy—clumsy, because we needed other agencies, as we didn't have the manpower or the will to watch too closely. And they didn't always see the need to share with us immediately or without politicking or bargaining.

So it was that we didn't hear for three days of a guarded phone call from Bulgaria to the Embassy. Apparently, Cheltenham had logged an iffy call but had only sent a précis out through normal channels. Smithy was immediately on the phone to Cheltenham, icily polite, browbeating the director until that worthy promised the original tape of the log, by courier. Less than six hours later, a very polite Triumph motorcycle-mounted courier drew up at the guardhouse at Mugglesby and handed tape and transcript personally to Smithy. The call was long-distance, in Bulgarian and guarded. The transcript ran:

"Mr Oblemov please."

"Who's speaking?"

"Pan Czerwony" (Mr Red).

"A minute."

(Pause)

"Oblemov."

"Czerwony."

"What do you want?"

"Your representative proved unsatisfactory. The goods were not as ordered. Substandard."

"Where is our representative?"

"Not here. Not anymore. Taking a bath."

"I see. What do you want?"

"My original order fulfilling."

"Where can we meet?"

"I see no point. You have my office number."

"And your contract is no longer viable. It is terminated."

(Pause)

"I know rival firms who would be interested in my product. And your firm's product."

"Mr Czerwony, you are in no position to threaten us. However, we will be in touch."

(Transmission terminates Z 15.30 hours.)

11

THE GABBLE OF BULGARIAN ON THE TAPE MEANT NOTHING TO ME, except the basso gravel of the voice—Kowalski. And those spavined, bureaucratic, lame-brained civil servants at GCHQ had left this for three days; had not traced Kowalski's call; had given it no follow-up. No wonder UK Intelligence is the laughing stock of the spy world. Only the Yanks can do worse.

Smithy and I immediately and furiously bashed out a précis of what we needed and phoned it through to our Beloved Führers. We demanded a twenty-four-hour-a-day electronic watch on the Bulgarians: R/T, W/T, and all the sophisticated gadgetry as well. We also put red-priority on Bulgarian phone calls. Then we frustratedly went back to screening for possible moles.

Three eye-boggling days later, just when I was losing the will to live, we hit gold: another phone call to the Bulgarians from Kowalski, traced to a public phone box in the Wakefield Ridings Centre. Once again, there was the grizzly-bear growl of Kowalski versus the smooth diplomatic tones of a career diplomat. Kowalski was beginning to get rattled, if anything that Neolithic can rattle. He did not sound happy.

The English transcript had him asking—*demanding*—his hard-earned cash and free passage to Poland or East Germany. Eventually, the Bulgarian reluctantly agreed to meet. It was arranged for the café section of the Ridings Centre in Wakefield at 15.30 the next day; out of Kowalski's stamping ground, and miles from the embassy. Kowalski must be feeling threatened to agree to meet in such an open and obvious place.

Smithy, punctilious as always, made effusive noises of gratitude at Cheltenham's response for being a bit less sluggish this time but still injecting a gentle *pulex irritans* in its collective ear. He collected me, Alan, and Ken, and in nil time flat, I was driving the Capri up the A1 like we had hornets after us. We booked in the Ridings Hotel. Then, armed with .38 S&Ws and radios, we began a close watch on the Ridings Centre, just in case the time and day were coded. *What if the place was coded as well?* I carefully didn't ask …

But, thankfully, the breaks went our way, because at 3.24 precisely, an open-faced, open-shirted young guy asked for a coffee in a vaguely mid-European accent. Sure, nothing strange about that—West Yorkshire is full of Polacks, Ukies, etc. But there was enough here to trigger alarms. I was covering the area at the time, and I buzzed Smithy, Alan, and Ken. Then I deliberately looked back to my *Guardian* crossword, filling in the spaces with my thumbnail description of Matey. Out of the corner of my eye, I saw Ken and Alan—a couple of rough labouring-types window-gazing— and Smithy camply dressed in tartan flares, pink shirt, and peach-coloured scarf mincing round the place.

At 3.36, the glass lift bottomed, and out of it stepped Kowalski, looking as near upset and haggard as a monolith can—unshaven, tacky hair, and he seemed to have lost weight. He looked hunted and less assured somehow. At bay, at risk, so twice as dangerous.

He circled the area. My heart paused. What if he recognised me or Smithy? But Smithy ghosted behind a pillar, and I buried myself in the *Guardian*, and the wary bull gaze moved on as he perched like a two-ton butterfly in front of the mid-European. The mid-European gentleman very carefully sat Kowalski down with a table-width between them.

We decided we daren't risk a long-range mike, so we had no idea what was said, but it was brief, with Kowalski demanding and the young man smiling, smarmy, pseudo-reasonable. Finally, he handed Kowalski a plastic carrier bag and stood up. Outwardly affable now, Kowalski backed out, stepped into the exit, and walked smartly away. Ken and Alan followed, leapfrogging.

Me and Smithy followed our new friend by the same means. Buddy-boy wandered round Wakefield for two hours, doing all the routine tail-dropping things, whilst Smithy and I stuck to him like an Aberdonian to a 3d bit. Finally, he caught the 6.05 London Express, and after a phone call to a mate of mine at the Yard, was safely tagged home, snug in the arms of … guess where? The Bulgarian Embassy.

Meanwhile, Ken and Alan ghosted Kowalski round and round Wakefield until dark. Café to pub, pub to café. Then, as Ken was tailing Alan tailing Kowalski up an alley at the side of the shops, he saw nothing until he fell over a heap of rags he finally recognised as Alan when the swearing began. Kowalski, using that animal-like sixth sense of his, had tagged Alan and zapped him, then disappeared into thin air.

Kowalski was really getting to be a pest. An obvious baddie, with a mind like a vaselined snake, eyes like a hawk with binoculars, and the strength of a couple of hypertrophied gorillas. And an ethical sense that would make an alley cat blush with shame. Back in the hotel, we Elastoplasted Alan's head and debriefed.

"He's taking a bit of catching, is Kowalski," I mused, "and even if we get him, we're going to have to sweat as hard as him to get him to cough."

"Yes," Smithy answered, "and even if he talks, where does that leave us? This is a ramshackle outfit, but surely they're not so stupid as to not have a cut-out. Even when we get him, we'll only be one step further on. Nonetheless, we can't leave an animal like this wandering around for too long. I wonder if he got his heart's desire for a passport and an Eastern Bloc visa. I really must meet Mr Kowalski, as soon as I can manage. He'd be interesting to talk to."

When Smithy talked like that, all sort of dreamy and faraway and gentle, he was at his most dangerous. And when Smithy met Kowalski, for all Kowalski's bulk and street wisdom, it wasn't Smithy I'd feel sorry for.

I looked around at the four of us: all Special Forces and sneaky-beaky background, all skilled, intelligent, and able. And a poncy little outfit ramshackle enough to use World War II radios has us by the short and curlies. We seemed up the creek without a paddle, whilst a nasty little Eastern European–invented terror group jumped around and blew people up as they felt fit.

I went back to the bar for another Guinness and cogitated moodily. I was professionally piqued. I longed to feel collars and to put our Bulgarian-inspired friends out of business. As I turned to the table, I caught the tail end of one of Smithy's manic, awful, and totally clean jokes,

"So she said, 'It's all in the grass hut,'" followed by lunatic laughter. Smithy's mood had swung into the manic. His brain was back up to speed and on the move again. Good! I'd get to feel collars yet!

Eventually, we turned in, stuck in double rooms, but not before Smithy had spent an expensive twenty minutes on the phone to Karen.

I awoke next morning to see Smithy, as usual on his knees with his black book, but after about five minutes he looked up and said, "Morning, Bill. I'm off for a jog, then after breakfast we're off down the road to Mugglesby, and Ken and Alan are off to London."

"But what about Kowalski?"

"He can wait. Sea-routes and airports are on the watch for him."

"But what if the Bulgarian got him a passport?"

"He'll turn up eventually. Nothing that big and ugly can stay hidden too long. And when he does, this time we'll have him."

I nodded intelligently. "So what do we do then?"

"We cover that embassy tighter than a Yorkshireman's wallet, electronically and physically. We get back to our suspect list. And when the two come together, we ... wait."

"Uh-huh, and where does that get us?"

"That gets us to the *fons-et-origio* of this lot."

At ten o'clock, we met in Ken and Alan's room. We split our marching orders. Smithy and I would arrange the electronic net, whilst Ken and Alan would arrange physical surveillance with a handful of grudgingly lent SIB detectives. I knew at least one of them, and SIB owed me a favour or two, so they would immediately supply me with any detail of other possible Bulgarian intelligence personnel. Then Ken, Alan, and SIB would sew them up tighter than a bug in a blanket. After a short wait whilst I telephoned our requirements through to our Faceless Führers and listened to their moans, we sped on our respective ways.

She was sick. She noticed her glasses no longer were quite as efficient. She was getting quite clumsy and dizzy. She was twitchy, and when she looked in the mirror, she noticed slight bumps on her face. She managed to hide these from her complaisant husband and social circle, playing Lady Bountiful and dutiful wife. But the rage burned: rage against a corrupt system that murdered and crippled so many people, especially her beautiful Polish flight lieutenant. Their day would come.

The next day, arriving back in our cell in Mugglesby, we'd set up an electronic surveillance on the Bulgarian Embassy from the section covering R/T, W/T, teleprinter, and all the known high-tech communications aids. The Mugglesby CO was again making grumbling noises about our pirating all his best operators, but Smithy had carte blanche, and there wasn't a lot he could do. Ken, Alan, and a handful of SIB blokes, in the meantime, had put twenty-four-hour surveillance on the embassy: very close, very discreet, very technical. And with the nuts and bolts in place, Smithy and I returned to our eyeball-aching scrutiny of suspects.

After much eye strain, boredom, and coffee, we got the list down to a dozen possibilities and three very hopefuls. First was another expatriate Pole, a guy called Bynowsky: ex-free Polish Air Force; worked as a rep for a Lancashire radio-parts wholesaler; vaguely knew Kowalski; spoke Bulgarian (which we thought Kowalski probably didn't); and was suspected of low-grade intelligence-gathering for the Eastern Bloc. Certainly the poor louse had enough relatives back in Poland to have the pressure put on him by Papa Bear, like a lot of the expatriates. He had worked on the Liverpool docks for a while and looked good for our spook.

The second suspect was a journalist, very left-wing. Sam Hardwick wrote freelance for locals and nationals, had flown bombers as radio op in the war, and had worked on the Manchester *Guardian* before it went national and trendy. Quite Conservative in his writings, but Five were fairly certain Hardwick was still passing low-level military intelligence, this time to East Germany. Possible; Sam had never really made the big time, as a reporter or a spy. The stuff he gave the DDR was fed to him by Five and was only routine handouts available to anyone. SIB and Five left him at it because he had some valuable DDR contacts they didn't want to lose sight of, especially in these days of very cold war.

Thirdly and most bizarrely was a large poshly spoken English lady, Sandra Stephens. Sandra had had no obvious connection other than a penchant to hang around the Free Forces in the war when she was a

WAAF signaller. A camp bicycle, we'd have called her. She had a child, several bouts of gonorrhoea, and an enduring moral hangover. She had been married to a Free Polish flight lieutenant who had—so surprise me—been killed in the same crash in which George Gregson had been so badly burned. She had apparently turned moral and religious, working long hours in rehabilitation camps after the war; had stood two terms as Conservative councillor in a West Lancs. town; and had sent her son to Merchant Taylors school to be made into a perfect little snob.

But the sneaky-beakies had doubts about several of her contacts— semi-clandestine meetings with very left TU officials and iffy contacts from her rehab work. She had married again—a David Stephens, an undertaker of all things. It seemed an odd combination for a spy, but the computer reported that she was fluent in most Slavic languages, including Bulgarian and Polish, and had had several open and above-board meetings with Bulgarians and clandestine meetings with minor criminals, all in the name of peace. All of which which was supposedly because of her rehabilitation and reform work, but the computer had its doubts. Cynical computers, yet! Whatever next?

"Well, Bill, which one do you fancy?"

"I don't know. I'm not for the woman, but the others seem a bit too obvious."

"But aren't this lot obvious? Aren't they so obvious, old-fashioned, and bludgeoning that they take us all by surprise?"

"Um, maybe. So why don't we put all three of 'em under surveillance? And we shouldn't forget the other hopefuls."

"If we can get the quality of operator. We're wearing out our welcome and our budget with the Bill, and we don't want any pointed blue heads poking over hedges and frightening 'em."

"Listen, Smithy, I'm in contact with a private firm. Basically security consultants, but not above a bit of counterespionage if the conditions demand it. Very pricey but very honest and discreet. And I've done them a favour or two in the past. The boss is a lad called Donald Grey—ex–chief super from the Met. Should I ring him?"

"Yes! Bill, this could be the answer. Hang on!"

Short break while Smithy rings London. Short stilted conversation. Smile of triumph from Smithy. "OK, Bill—the Führers will wear it."

I rang Donald Grey, and amazingly got him first time. I made all the recognition signals, went through all the how's-the-wife-and-brats-at-Winchester chat, and came away having traded £100-a-day of your and my PAYE for an agreement for a super-pussyfoot eyeballing on our Three Wise Monkeys, with daily reports to me personally.

So then it was hurry up and wait. We had our daily reports from the fuzz in the search for Kowalski. We gave our daily non-reports to Whitehall, and we built card-houses. We got reports from Ken and Alan on the goings-on at the embassy, from our own operators on the state of phone and radio traffic from the embassy, from Grey on the innocent-looking suspects we had sniffed out, and from Smithy after his daily phone call to Karen. And all (except, from Smithy's point of view, Karen's call) was negative.

We found out that Kowalski might have melted and run down the drain for any whisper of him. We found out the shopping lists of the whole embassy. Amazing how much decadent Western ice cream and burgers this lot ate. We found out that Bynowsky had a girlfriend, Hardwick had a boyfriend, and Mrs Stephens had two spaniels and an impeccable private life.

And as the monthly date for our outbreak of violence grew closer again, so tension increased.

She woke up screaming. Not with fear. Hate. Hate clawed at her guts. Hate was to her what once the love of men had been. And one in particular. Her darling. Her White Knight. Her One who had died. Horribly, horribly burned. He had been the torch that had ignited the rest of her life.

War! What was war? Obscene giants fighting each other, whilst people, real people, burned alive to sate them. Once she had thought of fliers as warriors, brave and noble. Not now. Now she knew they were dupes. Mugs. Conned. She knew that as long as bureaucracies governed and bullied everyone, more young men would burn.

It was natural, almost heaven-sent, when she was offered a job by a young mid-European who had offered it on behalf of the International Peace Movement, even though she knew people would suffer. That was a pity, of course, but what were a few lives to fight the hateful, many-sided monsters that were all governments? She had suffered, and now so must they. The hate must be assuaged.

She got up. She looked in the mirror. Without makeup, her face looked raddled, eaten, dissolving. They had told her that her beloved had given her syphilis, but that was a lie. How could he—brave, fearless, a lover as only a European could be. How could he? And he had burned! Burned!

Herself burning up with rage, she dressed, looked at the now-useless radio receiver, called the dogs, and went out to the public phone.

12

THREE DAYS LATER, A CAR BLEW UP IN A MULTI-STOREY CAR PARK IN York. There was no cut-and-dried connection with our friends, but it was the day before the usual D-day, there were no other major disasters, and the three people carrying the bomb (who, incidentally, were shredded) had no obvious links with any terrorist organisation; they were just petty and violent local criminals. It was not their regular *modus operandi*. They were more likely to mug old ladies on pension day or put the frighteners on small shopkeepers.

So maybe they had been hired and been just a bit inexperienced and clumsy. So maybe, just maybe, our malefactors were showing flaws. Just maybe our harassment was beginning to produce cracks in the monolith. Efficiency, never very good, just maybe was slipping.

We were still sitting around collating reports. All seemed negative. We widened our net and set a team of psychiatrists, counsellors, and therapists on to George Gregson, but that poor, alcohol-ridden, LSD-burned brain seemed to have given up any sort of coherence. George himself had settled down into a dreamy trance-like vegetating state in his safe ward in Bristol. Which was bully for him, but not a lot of use for us.

Kowalski also stayed disappeared in the fourth dimension. Neither hide nor hair of him could be found. And so we kept our filaments out, we kept blurring our vision on the useless reports cluttering our cell in Mugglesby, and we kept hoping for a break. Frustration on frustration. This cack-handed mob was, elusively, just out of our reach. Surely it couldn't last.

Because we didn't have any options, we kept reading reports on George, on Kowalski, on our three new suspects. Although Bynowski and Sam both had reasons to keep under any radar, they were fairly innocent. Bynowski made no contact with any clandestines but drank in an innocuous English pub or the Polish club. Sam slipped in and out of gay bars but otherwise was totally obvious.

Then a routine report from Grey's told us that Sandra Stephens had placed one phone call from an outside box three days before the bomb debacle. She had spent something like twenty minutes in the box, with her two dogs tied up outside. We had no record of what she said—apparently £100 a day isn't enough to provide tele-microphones—but it was a pointer. What's wrong with her home phone?

Smithy dived on it like a cormorant after a fish. "Now, Bill, why indeed would Sandra bother to phone from outside? She has a perfectly good phone at home, and we have a perfectly good tap on it. She knows something!"

"Maybe a bit far-fetched, Smithy. Perhaps she has a lover and doesn't want Undertaker David to know. Maybe she forgot something until she was out!"

"Maybe, but it's a straw worth grabbing at. She'll repay a little more thorough investigation, I think."

"So who?"

"So me and you."

"So when?"

"What's wrong with tonight?"

Thus, after a typical forces meal in the Mugglesby officers' mess, we departed for the North West again. We arrived in Presborough, Sandra's stamping ground, about five-thirty—just in the rush hour. Sandra's pad was detached, in a quiet cul-de-sac, and oozing money. Who said undertaking was a dying trade? Not an easy place to keep surveillance on; Grey's men had resorted to the tired old chestnut of a little red van, a small tent, and a lifted manhole cover, with a little transistor radio innocuously turning out Radio Caroline. Smithy and I found Millets on the point of closing and bought a couple of pairs of overalls, flat caps, and big boots.

Then we relieved Grey's men and sat gazing at the Stephens domicile, willing it to do something. And at eight o'clock, it did: it disgorged the two Stephenses, Mercedes mounted, poshly dressed, and shot them town-wards.

We waited till it was dark and then ghosted out of the hole and into the house. We shaded up to a set of patio doors, and I took out a set of strictly illegal instruments. A brief instant of fiddling, a grunt of success, and the patio doors slipped silently back. Give the Stephenses their due: expensive, money-no-object patio doors never gave us an easier time. And give them their due as well: the oh-so-obvious, bright yellow burglar alarm box was empty.

We phantomed around the place by the dimness of penlight torches, materialising and dematerialising from room to room, always looking for any clue to prove or disprove Sandra's involvement with Bulgaria.

We found out that the Stephenses had separate bedrooms.

And we found out that in Sandra's was a clumsily hidden radio transmitter. It was an old tank-set, built into a dressing table and powered by a 12v train-set transformer. We photographed it and made a careful note of type, placement, and even the frequency it was set on, just in case Sandra had been careless.

Eureka! Now we could really move. We'd sew her up tighter than an Irishman on Saturday night. We'd get a warrant to search her mail— incoming and outgoing; get Mugglesby to sit on her transmitter frequ; and try to provoke her into reaction. I could see Smithy's pale smile of satisfaction in the glow-worm of the torch as he nodded us door-wards. We ghosted backwards, closing up and covering up as we went, back to the patio doors.

Smithy spectred his way out—and suddenly dropped, poleaxed. I saw a shadowy figure looming in the doorway and attacked. A front-fist strike was parried expertly, a low snap kick missed, and I only managed to parry a head blow with difficulty and loss of breath and dignity. This was no mean opponent.

The fight gasped and panted out into the garden, neither Shadow nor I able to score decisively, but for myself, basic unfitness was beginning to show. Then suddenly, it was all over. With no rational volition from him, and no help from me, Shadow suddenly levitated to head height with a startled whoosh of breath and descended with a dislocating crunch. Smithy was obviously back in action.

I dived on his legs; Smithy smothered his torso and put a stranglehold on him. Even then, Shadow was not easy. He was muscly and trained, and he fought and wriggled desperately. Eventually, the struggles grew faint, and Shadow slept.

We were in a bit of a quandary. We were here running light, without backup. So we couldn't whistle up a van to sweep up the sleeper. Nor in a quiet, upper-middle-class neighbourhood can one walk round carrying unconscious hooligans—not without being noticed, you can't. And there's a very finite time that you can stand, Cerberus-like, on guard over a Sleeping Beauty in someone else's garden.

So we tied his thumbs together with his own shoelaces, gagged him with his own handkerchief, and slapped his face softly and repeatedly until he came round. Then, when he stirred, we briskly lifted him to his feet, frogmarched him out to the van, and radioed Grey's men to take back over. Then we drove him in our own car to the local police station, waved our warrant cards, and borrowed a cell.

Then we got down to interrogation. And what a surprise, because Matey was wearing a dog collar. At first, I was very suspicious: no better disguise, no better excuse for coming and going, no more disarming role to play than that of a vicar. *Dead giveaway*, I thought, for I remembered what a fight this guy had put up. It was like holding down a bag of panthers. And where do you get a real vicar who's a tough, trained martial artist from?

Smithy removed the gags and shoelaces and started on interrogation. The talk became a meaningless mumbo jumbo of theology, and when Matey produced a card with "Rev. D. Atkinson" on it, Smithy finally pronounced himself satisfied.

However, Rev. D. was not so easily mollified. He doubted the reality of our ID cards, and he refused to believe Sandra could be a suspected terrorist. She was one of his stalwarts—in fact, he had been delivering something charitable to her when he had seen our torches (careless, that) and set an ambush. But how could a suburban vicar have the observation to notice our torches, or the know-how to mount such a devastating ambush, much less the bottle to put it into effect?

Easy, explained Rev. D. (by now, he and Smithy were on "John" and "Derek" terms; all these God-botherers are like the Masons without a funny handshake). He had been converted while a second lieutenant in the Paras, had done a tour of duty with the SAS, and had only trained as a vicar later. "And a pity I'm out of condition and practise, or I'd had given you two a run for your money," he said, smiling ruefully.

Smithy grunted, also ruefully; fingered a bump the size of a bantam egg behind his ear; and decided that the vicar's condition and practise was all right by him, thanks all the same.

Eventually, we convinced Rev. D. that we had real, non-fictional grounds for suspecting Sandra of naughtiness, and we invoked the seal of the confessional or whatever on him plus the Official Secrets Act, D-notices, and anything else we could think of. As no charge had been laid with the blue-pointed-head mob, we just opened the door on Rev. D., and he and Smithy stood on the doorstep shaking hands and promising further meetings at the prayer mat or the judo mat whilst the local plods looked on gobsmacked, and who can blame them? Two clandestines with national clout hustle a vicar trussed up like a turkey, pulling all sorts of strings, yet a short half-hour later are all buddy-buddy with the ex-turkey.

In the meantime, Smithy recruited Rev. D. to keep an eye on Sandra and elicited a promise to phone.

"I'm looking forward to a bit of clandestine again," said Rev. D., a fiendish glow behind his eyes. Then the glow turned wistful. "Sometimes I think I'm not as converted as I ought to be!"

"None of us are," Smithy replied, also looking wistful. "None of us are."

Two idiots meet in the dark, fight each other stupid, one gets knocked out, the other gets tied up and interrogated, and then they trust each other. I mean, to the extent that the Official Secrets Act gets torn up by the one, and the other puts his vicarly reputation and dignity on the line, as well as any chance to make bishop, to spy on one of his most philanthropic and influential parishioners, all on the others' say-so. Crazy!

Despite my heated protests, Smithy gave Rev. D. Atkinson the Mugglesby number, the Whites' number, and Grey's number. And when I asked on what possible grounds he dared do that, he left me gobsmacked by simply saying, "Deep calls to deep, Bill lad, deep calls to deep," and stalking off smiling.

Sometimes these muscular Christians can get very wearing!

It's amazing, this case. A ramshackle outfit of second-class desperados and a posh upper-middle-class woman continue to run rings around an experienced, hand-picked, and government-backed anti-espionage team. The team leader ends up in hospital, stabbed and poisoned; we struggle all over the street in Liverpool 8 with a half-caste lady judo expert; and finally we get mugged by a vicar. This really was too much. I was feeling very stupid, very embarrassed, and very angry now. I stomped down the steps after Smithy, who magnificently ignored the open mouths or sly grins of the local constabulary.

As soon as we'd booked into a hotel, we phoned Grey's to tell them where we were at and to leave a number where we could be contacted. We turned in early, in a double room again, and the last thing I remember is Smithy on his knees with his black book.

It seemed no time at all—in fact, it *was* no time at all—before we were awakened by a banging on the door. "Urgent phone call for Mr Smith, urgent phone call for Mr Smith" called the night porter, grumpy and sleepy, taking his spite out on the door. Even in the middle of the night, we were not going to be taken by surprise and rose from our beds like a pair of ghosts, Smithy nodding at me to take position behind the door as he drifted towards it. He opened the door with a silent rush, but it was only the night porter, whiffing irritatedly through his walrus moustache, "Phone for Mr Smith downstairs!"

Smithy was gone about five minutes and came back into the room looking very pale and concerned. It seemed that Karen had come face to face with Kowalski in Liverpool 8 and was certain that he had made her from the time she and Smithy had spent in Kowalski's local. Notwithstanding this, she had followed him until she lost him in a maze of demolition work. Then she had run home, phoned Mugglesby, and been given the typical RAF run-round—but by getting in touch with Grey's, she got in touch with us. All this had taken hours, and Smithy was in quite an uncharacteristic fluster, dithering and flapping. Amazing what a woman can do.

"Right," said I. "Let's get Karen out; I think up here would be safest, and let's send Henry and Molly White on holiday for a month. Kowalski may be a loner, but he's a wild, dangerous, unpredictable loner. He's just as likely to take out the whole White family on the off-chance as blink. We can't take any chances."

Suiting deed to word, I rang a contact in the Devon and Cornwall constabulary to arrange a hotel in Torquay next morning. Thankfully, he was on shift. Then I rang the Whites, told Karen to drive up here right away, no messing about, and told her parents they were on holiday, all expenses paid, on the government, WEF tomorrow. Then I booked Karen in the next room to us.

Finally, I went back to the room and assured Smithy that everything was under control.

"Thanks, Bill. I'm sorry I went to pieces. I didn't fancy Karen near that big ape. Still, being a wally wouldn't help her."

After two hours, Karen went down to the kitchen and smilingly charmed old Walrus-Features into making us a cup of tea, unpacked in her room, then came into ours. She and Smithy coiled round each other like a pair of boa constrictors, and I ghosted out of the room before I got too green and hairy. I tried my charms on Walrus-Features, but it didn't work until I got out the flask. Only Teacher's, but it soothed and mollified him, and he was quite interesting on the subject of World War II, the government, and the price of ciggies, until I decided that Smithy had had a long-enough snog.

The wild bull had returned. Cautiously sniffing the air for danger, every sense alerted and sharpened, every ganglion standing on end, Kowalski unhurriedly unlocked his flat door, breathed a sigh of relief, and reached into the fridge for a cold beer.

I am invincible, he thought. *The Germans couldn't beat me. The Russians couldn't beat me, so neither these soppy rule-bound British nor those inefficient Bulgarians have a chance. The British, despite that long streak of govno with the nunchaku, are too polite and soft, while as for those Bulgarians—second-class James Bonds, every one of them. Fancy thinking they could take ME out with an old gag like the poisoned umbrella. Well, at least one of them knows better by now.*

So the wild bull was back. Staying with relatives or compatriots was all very well, but tongues vibrate and whispers take wings, and back on

Merseyside he was on his own ground, fighting in his own territory, and look out anyone who got in his way.

But what about that black dolly-bird? He was sure he'd seen her with the nunchaku-basher. And he sensed the recognition in her eyes. Then he knew it for certain when she followed him. He had led her a merry dance across Liverpool 8 until he deliberately lost her in a building site. At any one point, he could have jumped her and showed her what a real man is like, but he was playing a longer game. So he had followed her home, noted her address, and gone to his bed-sit to plan his reprisal. Tomorrow, they would know ... the wild bull had returned.

He unhurriedly left his flat, walked steadily and gorilla-like down the road, and entered his local boozer, where he'd first seen the black bird and the nunchaku-artist. Grunting hellos to this one and that, he hove up to the bar. Looking round through the Woodbine haze, he signalled to two guys at the far end of the bar. They obediently shambled forward, one skinny, dressed in what had been a sharp suit, now stained with tobacco ash and beer; the other muscular but fat from too many pub pies and too much beer. He was dressed in blue jeans and a T-shirt, tight across his gut.

"Daren," he nodded to Skinny. "Marcus," to Fatty. "I have a leetle job for you. One you'll enjoy." He smiled and moved his hands a few inches apart.

"Sure, Kowy, usual pay?"

"A bit more for this one: twenty-five."

"Each?"

"Yah, each"

"What is it?"

"A kidnapping. There's a black whore been in here too often, wants to know too much about my business." Giving Darren her address, he rumbled, "Get a taxi—nick it from Lime Street, go to this address, and knock for her. When she answers, give 'er some of this"—he passed over a little brown bottle and a none-too-clean handkerchief—"and bring her back here." *And when I get her*, he smiled inwardly, *I will have some Polish fun—the sort the Gestapo and the KGB used to have with our Polish women.*

Karen stealthily moved out of her parents' flat, gingerly closing the door. She had left a note explaining what was going on, and that Bill would be in touch. She cautiously scoped the road. Good—no big ugly Poles. Then she stepped out as she caught sight of the taxi.

"Exchange Station, please," she said as she hurried inside.

"Oh, yer won't be goin' there!" chortled a small, smelly man.

"Yer sure won't!" grinned a fat smelly man. Before she knew what was happening, the fat man produced a grubby handkerchief smelling of hospitals and clapped it over her nose and mouth. She slept.

She awoke lying on a dusty sofa, arms and legs tied with window cord, with a head clanging like a fire bell and two plug-uglies leering and breathing halitosis at her.

"Welcome back, sweetheart. Yer've gorra appointment with Mr Kowalski. Black whore, he said get, and ..." triumphantly, "black whore we've got!"

"Hey, Marcus!" jabbered Skinny. "Kowy won't be back for hours! A bit of extra pay for me 'n' you! What d'yer reckon?"

Marcus seemed initially hesitant, but then his bloated features lit up. "Yeh! Never 'ad a black bird!"

Karen's muzzy head was gradually clearing. She'd heard the dreaded K-word, and she knew if that big ape got his hands on her, she wouldn't get out alive. She croaked, "I gorra pee!"

"Do it there!" snarled Marcus.

"Kowalski won't be happy with a wet sofa," she whimpered.

"OK, we'll untie your legs—not yer ain't gerrin yer hands free."

Obediently, she trotted off to the disgusting bathroom, kicked the door shut, and settled herself as best as she could. As she did so, a plan formed.

She let herself with difficulty back into the living room. Now, it all depended on Kowalski not coming back too soon.

"Hey, guys, I could do with a cupper tea!" she whined.

"It'll cost yer!" smirked Darren.

"I've got no money on me."

Darren smirked again.

"OK, I'd kill for a cupper tea," she gasped. "And I can pay yer. But with me 'ands tied?"

Gormless Marcus found a kitchen knife and slit her bonds.

"Now, who's first?" Karen paused, "Eeny-meeny-miney mo ... You," pointing to Darren.

She wiggled her hips, lay back on the sofa, and hitched up her skirt. Daren was on her like an odiferous fox on a rabbit.

She wrapped her legs so tightly round his waist he couldn't move, then applied a sliding-collar strangle. Marcus was jealous of Darren's frantic jerks and didn't notice his friend turning purple. When he was still, she jumped up. "You next!" she cried. Seizing Marcus by the hair, she kicked him in his tumescent member, pulled his head down, and kneed him in the face. He too slept.

Then Karen was violently sick. Finding nothing to clean herself up with, she spat, grabbed her handbag, and ran out. Flagging down another taxi, she gasped, "Exchange station! Quick!"

Smithy was beginning to worry. "Karen's late!" he told the window. "What's keeping her?"

I tried to reassure him, but he was right—she was late.

At long last, a taxi drew up, and out shot a dishevelled Karen. Smithy ran down the stairs three at a time and hugged her, stroking her sick-covered hair.

"What's happened?" he bawled. "Why are you like this?"

"Kowalski!" said Karen, and fainted

Smithy carried her upstairs, by which time she was coming round. "Hey! Is this a harbinger of things to come?" she smiled groggily but humorously.

She then disappeared in the shower for about forty minutes. "I had to get the stink of those two off," she said as she reappeared, looking tired but smiling. "Am I glad to see you!"

"That Kowalski shall most certainly pay for this," mused Smithy reflectively. I bit down any remark about *vengeance is mine* as inappropriate.

Smithy and Karen immediately wrapped around each other

After coughing discreetly and knocking, I pushed my head round the door. Smithy and Karen were twined round each other still but had surfaced for air and were sitting up and taking notice.

"Smithy," I suggested, "how's about you and I follow-up Kowalski, and Karen helps out keeping Sandra Stephens under close scrutiny? And, I've had a thought."

"Careful, Bill!" Karen chortled. "It's only Friday!"

I stuck my nose in the air and snootily said, "For that, you can wait! Wait till we've found a caff and filled up."

When we were sure Karen was quite recovered, we went to look for an early-opening café and found one down road. There we replenished our inner persons with the largest orgy of cholesterol we could find: sausages galore, fried bread, mushrooms, tomatoes, beans, and rasher after rasher of bacon—of course, with toast and marmalade and gallons of hot, strong Lancashire tea.

Then we rolled back to the hotel room to plan and digest.

"Now, I've been thinking," I began.

"Careful, Bill," smiled Karen.

Loftily ignoring her, but glad to see her back on form, I continued, "We've got Sandra sewn up as to comings and goings," I mused, "but we need to get closer to her. Maybe you and I, Smithy lad, could cultivate David, but I don't think he's aware of what his missus is up to. So— quiet, Karen," I growled. "Now my idea: What is Sandra? Retired local councillor, doyen of the WI, the bridge club, and the golf club. So she's a snob—a parish-pump Lady Muck. And who do we know who's middle class, professional, and a high-powered business woman? Who could easily get close to Sandra?"

I paused and presented with a flourish, "Nessie!"

Smithy wasn't sure, but Karen thought it a great idea: "Yes, from what you tell me, Bill."

"But we do need to get close to Sandra. We've no real evidence. Having a tacky old radio transmitter is not illegal. And she does have a lot of local friends and clout."

"Go on, Bill, keep the brain turning," encouraged Smithy.

"Well, as I said, you and I can't easily get close, we'd be way too suspicious and obvious; two strange blokes chatting up Sandra?"

"None stranger!" muttered Karen, poise and good humour quite regained.

Boy. She's one tough lass. I plodded on. "Karen is probably the wrong shade for a small-town prejudicial Conservative councillor like our Sandra, but who better than Nessie? She flies much higher than a small-town council, she's a Posh Bird; middle class; high-powered job; and cosmopolitan. Sandra'll be cultivating her like nothing on earth."

We kicked the idea around for a while, then finally all agreed it would be a great idea if she was available. As it was Friday night, I caught the express down to the Smoke to chat her up face to face. Only to ask her? Of course. I took her out to the local pizzeria and, feeling replete, she sighed, finished her wine, and sat back, "OK, Chief Superintendent Sneaky-Beaky, what are you after?"

"Who? Me?" I enquired innocently, halo gleaming.

"Yes, you! You're up to something. I know you well enough by now."

"Funny you should say that, sweetheart, but how do you fancy a holiday on the Costa del Lancashire? Geen hills, respectable company, and as many mill-chimneys as you can count?"

"Explain!"

So I told her chapter and verse of everything we had been up to, and why we needed a classy, gorgeous mole, ripping up the Official Secrets Act as I went. Bad influence, that Smithy.

"Well, work is a bit flat at the moment, and I could do with a bit of excitement." I looked hurt. "So let's do it!" she carolled, ignoring me.

After spending Saturday with me trying to give her the excitement she claimed to lack, she phoned her boss, gave him a great porky about needing to rush up north to a poorly granny, packed, and said, "Tell me more!"

I clued Nessie in about the way Sandra was behaving, who and what she was, and the class-riddled locals she mixed with, and asked her to make like the stuffiest and most conservative of Conservatives.

She continued excitedly, "And as I'm a buyer for a national company, maybe I should start rumours about commercial possibilities."

"Great! Appeal to class consciousness and cupidity," I enthused.

Then it was time to get to Euston.

When we arrived, Smithy and Karen were waiting. Thankfully, Karen and Nessie got on immediately, chatting away animatedly.

"Superb!" I chortled. "Now we've got it in black and white!"

Exchanging a severe look, Nessie and Karen reached out, each seized an ear, and twisted. Ouch! Then they turned to each other and grinned.

Repairing to the station caff, we breakfasted like Gargantua and kicked ideas round. "Nessie, you have business cards, no doubt," said Smithy. "So how's about you go along to see Undertaker David in his role as councillor and, without lying, explain who you are, who you work for, and that you're up here for a short break. And see if the fish bites?"

"You won't let me lie?" playfully grumped Nessie. "That's going to cramp my style! Remember what I do for a living."

Smithy just grinned.

We agreed to go back to the hotel and let me and Nessie shower the British Rail dust off ourselves, and Nessie put the warpaint on to go and see David. She dressed mid-morning coffee meeting: slim-cut expensive jeans, high-necked white not-too-severe T-shirt, beige cardigan, and low heels. Enough to make Undertaker David sit up but not to give him too many wandering thoughts. Which, being married to Sandra, I was sure he must have.

Within the hour, Nessie was back, grinning like a whole bagful of Cheshire cats. "Wow, that was easy! I think I should become one of your sneaky-beakies!"

"You already are," I grunted. "I could be shot at dawn three times over for spilling to you."

"Get away, Bill," chortled Karen. "You know you love her."

Smithy coughed meaningfully and glanced teasingly at me. "But now, kiddie-winkies, down to business."

"That was surprisingly easy," Nessie told us. "David is a gentle sort of guy, seems very much under Sandra's thumb and overawed by strong women. And he is looking for respect, which he doesn't get a lot of at home, I suspect. I also dangled my employer's credentials at him. Sorry, John, but I did lie a teensy-weensy bit about commercial prospects. So I've wangled a ticket for Karen and me for tomorrow night's council-anniversary ball. I'm sorry, Karen, I don't mean to be racist, but would you come as my patronised personal assistant?"

"Yessuh, ma'am," came a chocolate-soft African American voice, "us po' black folks is always ready to serve." A face-splitting grin robbed it of any offence or offensiveness.

Then the girls went off on a Nessie-funded shopping spree while Smithy and I got down to more plotting.

Next day we spent relaxing, going over to Blackpool, walking the Golden Mile, and gutsing on ice-creams and fish-'n'-chips.

Come the evening, after spending hours getting ready, two gobsmackingly, stunningly beautiful creatures swanned into our room— Nessie, clad in a mid-length Little Black Number, pearl choker, and stiletto heels with a Dusty Springfield hairdo, and Karen, more soberly dressed as befits the Serving Classes in a sober check pencil dress, mid-heels, and Western-cut flicked hair, with a string of ethnic beads, but still knocking our eyes out. Both had chosen outfits to make the most of their body types: Nessie well-built and stacked, Karen tall and proud and also stacked. I could see in Smithy's eyes how he felt. I reckon I looked the same.

When we had recovered, I asked them to be a bit circumspect round David—no flirting—but cultivate Sandra.

"Telling your grandma to suck eggs," scornfully replied Nessie. "My job is smooching hard-nosed sellers. It's what I do best."

Smithy and I went round to Rev. Derek's pad to keep him up to date. His wife welcomed us in—a slim, jeans-clad, vivid blonde bombshell of a vicar's wife, not a tweed skirt or twin-set to be seen.

"It's good to meet you guys. I know Derek loves being a vicar, and the church loves him, but sometimes I think he hankers after a bit more hooliganism. And …" she smiled, "what would the PCC think of brawling in a member's front garden with two clandestine thugs? Now I'll go and get the coffee."

We spent a convivial evening *chez* Atkinson, swopping tall tales of derring-do about our time in the Special Forces and wondering how the girls were getting on.

The girls returned at midnight, triumphant.

"We laid on the charm with a trowel to Sandra, admired her frumpy dress, and got her to tell us about her One True Love, a Polish flight lieutenant who died in a burned-out Lancaster; her successes with her work with rehabilitation; and how good a councillor she was. And how good it was to meet Someone of Her Own Class."

"That was Nessie, of course," Karen pointed out. "I just stayed in the background, suitably 'umble, and fought off the heavy-handed chat-ups of the local Hoorah Henries, some old enough to be my grandad. 'Ah's not a gurl lak dat. Ah'm promised to anodder.' And while Posh Bird here was being the life and soul, I lurked; my eyes, ears, and antennae were busily picking up things."

"However," Nessie continued, "some of the gossipy old ladies I talked to were a bit iffy about Sandra. Apparently, she'd had a bit of a riotous reputation as a local girl—despair of her very upright parents. They were relieved when she joined the WAAFs and came back a respectable Air Force officer's widow."

"Yes, that's more than what we already have, love," I interjected.

"But," Nessie resumed, "she is involved with some dodgy characters through her rehab. work."

Karen jumped in. "I went downstairs to talk to the hired help. And from what I overheard, there have been goings-on with them that David turns a blind eye to. Rehab, in its widest sense."

"That is very useful," said Smithy. "Tomorrow, I'll get on to the rehab charity and the local police to find out if she knows a plug-ugly called Kowalski. And well done, you private eyes."

Then we parted. I offered to save us some money by swopping Nessie and me to Karen's room and she move next door, but old-fashioned morality won out, and Smithy and Karen made a protracted regretful farewell at her door.

13

ARLY MONDAY MORNING, WE SET OUT BACK TO LIVERPOOL. IT WASN'T as early as I hoped, cos of course, Smithy had to say goodbye to Karen. You'd think she was going back home to Mars instead of across the Pennines. And the number of *goodbyes, take care, Johns, I will darlings,* etc., ad infinitem, certainly ad nauseam, took forever.

My goodbye to Nessie was much shorter, but she insisted with all her high-powered professional manner that she was kept strictly in touch.

"It's 'need to know'," I teased her.

"Well, I'm one of you now, *and I need to know!*" was her parting shot as the train pulled out.

Then we had to stick the local Lancashire Bill for a car Kowalski wouldn't make. It turned out to be an impounded, clapped-out, rusty wreck of an Austin 1100, B-reg, with an asthmatic engine to match. I certainly hoped Kowalski couldn't run too fast.

Of course, we hit the M6 traffic just right: bang in the middle of rush hour. After accelerating onto the southbound carriageway with the effortless power of a sloth with corns, we crawled down the county, fighting every inch of the way with juggernauts driven by blind and sadistic cobbalds and belching raw poison, as well as with yuppies proving that a Cortina can get glued to the bumper of an 1100.

So I fetched us up in Liverpool's dockland and outside the Whites' flat, with a stinging headache, enough tension to blow the Post Office Tower over, a bad temper, and a desire to strangle Kowalski, Smithy, the mongrel cocking its leg against our wheel, or anyone else in view.

My mood wasn't helped by Smithy reading his black book and praying all the way over. I knew he wasn't praying for protection, but I still felt it reflected on my driving.

After dropping Karen off at home we limped the old 1100 over the Snake Pass and ended up back in Sleaford six hours later, and into the local pub for a pint of Guinness and a therapeutic orange juice for Smithy.

Next day, we were back in Mugglesby, using their facilities, phoning Q, Five, and the Liverpool fuzz to search out the rehab group Sandra had adopted and any suspects or characters with form. I invoked the name of Sir Lindsey Attwaller, and, surprise, we had all three answers within twenty-four hours.

"Hey! Catch this, Smithy!" I gleefully shouted above the rattle of the teleprinter. "Guess whose name starting with K is on this list! Q and Five had had misgivings about our favourite plug-ugly. And Liverpool police had him on a very short list, but witnesses tended to disappear."

"Right, you ratbag!" Smithy ground out. "We'll have you. Well done, Bill, we're onto 'em!"

Giving a fond farewell to Mugglesby, hopefully for the last time, ears ringing to the COs farewell of "We don't want to miss you, but we think you ought to go," we pootled back to Liverpool.

Nessie still had some leave left, so she came up to be ops manager and link person for us.

Kowalski sat in his ratty apartment, cogitating. *I expect I've still got a job with that snotty posh bird up in Presbury,* he mused. *But to me now, this is personal. That long streak with the nunchaku, and that black bird pretending to be a whore, but I can see she's a black that's got above her station and thinks she can fool Kowalski. Pity I didn't get the finances off Posh Bird to afford better help. But I will get her; nobody disses the Wild Bull like this. And then I'll have Nunchaku by the short and curlies. Then we'll see who can win! And she might just be a bit of fun—for me, that is. She won't enjoy it! But she will take an experience with her to meet her Maker.* Kowalski was a long-lapsed Catholic, but the words stayed with him sometimes. *I will wipe out her whole family, just like the Gestapo wiped out mine.*

Kowalski was incandescent with rage, but in the back of his ice-brain— the ice-brain that had kept him alive and unscathed all these years—a plan was forming. *Simple is best,* he thought. *Too complicated, there's too much to go wrong. And Wild Bull does not go wrong.* The experience of finding two unconscious minions tied in window cord on his floor had dented his *amour propre* big-time. He had assuaged some of his anger on them, beating them almost back to unconsciousness and waving their fifty pounds in their faces before putting it back into his pocket, but his rage was still limb-shakingly incandescent even while the ice-brain plotted.

Smithy's ensemble this morning was grey hair; patched and stretched Crimplene trousers, too short and held up by a tie; shirt with a collar torn off; and an old hacking jacket with dubious stains on it that I daren't even guess at. And the smell! Smithy was a perfectionist, and I had been chased down the M6 by a miasma you could taste and almost see—consisting, as far as I dared try to identify it, of loose tobacco, stale urine, and human sweat. It didn't help my mood or my headache one bit, and I wondered how fastidious Smithy could bear walking round stinking like a polecat's poor relation.

He creaked out of the door, leaving his smell behind, clutching a paper bag, ostensibly with a half-pint but actually a walkie-talkie, and staggered down the road. I snuggled down in the 1100 to await events, to read the *Telegraph*, and to listen to the Stones on Radio Caroline. I saw Smithy collapse in a doorway, limbs scattered like jackstraws, and take a pull at his half pint.

"OK, Bill?" his voice crackled.

I turned the volume down and replied, "OK, Smithy."

With that scintillating dialogue, we settled down to the long boring job of waiting for Kowalski. As I fingered the safety catch of my good old S&W 0.38, I hoped wryly that Kowalski wouldn't be like Godot. I wanted that psychotic Polack. I wanted him banged up and the key thrown away—so badly my teeth ground. But gradually, tension eased, my headache got better, and concentration lapsed. It had been a hard night last night, and I felt my eyes go out of focus. The radio was now softly inviting me to go to San Francisco, wearing flowers in my hair. Sure. Just my barrow ... I dozed ...

A milk float buzzed down the road, stopping outside a pub. A shadow bulked large into the milkman's vision, and as he turned to smile, the lights went out. Bundling the unconscious milkman into the pub's alley, Kowalski slipped into the white coat, splitting the seams, and perched the cap precariously on his large head. He puttered off on the milk float, unpacking clinking bottles from his rucksack.

I watched the locals idly. A postman came and went, and a handful of dowdy women in curlers dragging scruffy toddlers wobbled past—a fair cross section of life in that area. A milk float purred up. Out of it climbed a huge milkman, overall tight across his shoulders. I jerked awake. Kowalski! I'd know that ugly bear anywhere.

He took a crate of bottles off the float. Only two of the bottles were milk-coloured. I was reaching for the transmitter-mike when I heard the receiver crackle.

"Bill, got him?"

"Right, Smithy, I'm on him!"

As Kowalski disappeared up the steps towards the Whites' flat, I greased out of the car. As I ghosted up the steps, Smithy floated up behind me. We turned onto the landing—just in time to see Kowalski empty one of his bottles through the White's letterbox and follow it with a cigarette lighter.

All hell broke loose. An eerie orange flare lit the landing. I pulled out the S&W and Smithy ran forward, screeching incoherently and fearsomely.

Kowalski turned and threw another bottle. Smithy leaped over the spreading liquid fire and hit Kowalski with the walkie-talkie. Kowalski grunted and hit Smithy in the short-ribs. Smithy gasped, pushed back by the force of the blow, but he grabbed Kowalski's fist. Blocking Kowalski's ankle with his foot, he threw Kowalski into the flames.

But before Smithy could disable Kowalski, he was up, unleashing a kick at Smithy's groin. Smithy turned and took it on the thigh, falling heavily. Immediately, Kowalski was on top of him, punching him viciously in the face.

Smithy grabbed him by the collar—*kata juji jime*, judo cross-strangle—and pulled Kowalski towards him, cutting off the air supply and immobilising his arms. I danced in over the flames, swinging the S&W at Kowalski's head … but with a huge heave of his shoulders, the ox pulled free. The S&W bounced off his skull and clattered along the landing. He snatched himself free, turned, and ran, jumping the fire.

"Oh, no, not this time, you don't," I shouted and threw one of his bottles at him. Unfortunately, this one was milk. He turned and gave a triumphant sneer, splashed in the white liquid. And that was his undoing. The next bottle, *not* milk, exploded in his face, covering him in liquid fire. As he screamed and turned, I raced to the S&W, pushed a dazed but rising Smithy out of the way, and deliberately shot Kowalski three times—double tap to the body and once, the coup de grâce, to the head. Jumping over the smoking corpse, I raced to the 1100 and put in an immediate call to the fire brigade, then collapsed, trembling, in the driving seat. Smithy appeared and collapsed in the passenger seat.

"Kowalski's dead, Bill."

"Can't pretend to be sorry, John."

"Me neither. I'll repent of that later."

We sat silent until the fire brigade and CID arrived. The detective sergeant was no one we knew—a portly, ulcer-ridden-looking guy with a surly and disbelieving expression. We were dragged into police HQ, and only after a bit of ID-waving and rank-pulling by me were we presented with a superintendent who'd worked with us and released us.

"Phew, Smithy, you don't half stink!" the super grinned. "New career as a dosser?"

Smithy grinned ruefully, "Earning me Oscar, Guv," he whined.

There would have to be an inquiry—I had shot a man dead, after all—but I trusted my striped-trousered Kaisers to get us out of it somehow. We climbed back into the 1100 and exhaustedly drove up to Presborough. One good thing at least: Smithy smelled only of fire now, instead of human waste and alcoholism.

When we arrived, Smithy disappeared into the shower. After a good half-hour of splashing, scrubbing, and more tuneless Beatles murdering and hymn-mangling, Smithy emerged, a vision of loveliness in light-blue trousers, moccasins, and polo shirt. Unfortunately, the effect was spoiled by the black eye and fat lip that were mementos of a no-longer-dangerous psychopath.

Karen, who had been waiting more-or-less patiently for at least twenty minutes, went mad at the sight of it. First, Smithy was harangued for being so stupid as to get into danger. Then I got it for letting him. Boy, for someone who never swore, Karen nonetheless had a masterly command of English.

But Smithy just smiled fondly, shook his head admiringly, and said, "Karen, you look beautiful when you're angry," making her seethe even more. Eventually, the tide turned. Karen slowed down, stopped, then broke down, flinging herself into John's arms, weeping. At that point, I left.

Smithy reappeared in our room about two hours later, looking slightly crumpled and still tunelessly humming hymns. Then, suddenly, he was all brisk efficiency. Karen followed him in, and the three of us plotted.

"I reckon we put the bite on Sandra," I suggested. "Spook her someway into getting rattled. Maybe she'll contact her minions."

"How?" asked Karen.

"I reckon if we work the old double-shuffle on her—one obvious follower and two or three not-so-obvious—that might work," I replied.

"Yes!" said Smithy, jumping up. "Yes—I reckon that might work."

"So who?" I asked. "We've run out of money for Donald Grey's lot."

"Well, Bill," said Smithy, "How's about Nessie invites her for coffee and drops hints about the need for peace, and what does she think of the way minorities are treated? When she leaves, I follow obviously, and you and the Sass lads play leapfrog and keep her sewn up tighter than a Yorkshire woman's purse."

At that, Smithy reached his arm for the phone and telephoned Mugglesby, where Ken and Alan were kicking their heels and making nuisances of themselves to the RAF. After a short, laconic conversation, Smithy put down the receiver and turned to us with a grin. "The lads are getting restless, moaning about us getting all the action, and saying it's about bloody time they got us out of our scrapes." Meanwhile, I phoned Q and got a tap put on all the public phones for a mile round Sandra's pad. And we waited.

It took about three days before Sandra was sure she was being followed. She had met her new friend Vanessa a few times for coffee and found that the young lady moaned constantly about global politics. Sandra warned Nessie that her "coloured servant" was somewhat disaffected.

"Yes, I know, she can be very uncooperative," moaned Nessie, mentally apologising to Karen, "but where can you get good help? I've had to claw for every bit of promotion and respect, and I can't count how many bosses expect me to give sexual quid pro quo for every crumb thrown my way. And the fat sluggy ugliness of it all!" she added, mentally apologising to her thin, uxorious, and perfectly courteous line manager.

Sandra wondered whether she should mention her Bulgarian friend but decided to leave it for now. She was a bit spooked.

"Do you know this area?" she asked Nessie. "For three days, a skinny gorilla of a man with atrocious taste in clothes, an eyepatch, and red hair has been following me."

Wait till I tell Smithy! Nessie inwardly chortled.

"Everywhere I go," Sandra continued, "he is behind me, twenty or thirty yards back, ducking into doorways when I turn. If I ever go on a bus, he goes upstairs. If I go into the ladies, he will be staring into a shop window nearby when I come out. Some sort of pervert."

Nessie clucked sympathetically, looked at her watch, paid for the coffee, and, promising to meet up again, left.

Thank goodness for a sympathetic ear, Sandra thought.

At first, she had thought it was her paranoia. Presborough wasn't a big town, and he was very noticeable. But when she took her dogs for a walk at ten o'clock at night and saw his rear elevation in a telephone box, she was certain. She took note of him: old-fashioned suit; box-collar; blue-striped tie; polished boots—not shoes, but toecap boots yet! That and his short-back-and-corners hairdo convinced her. He was the fuzz. He was a pig! Probably some just-about-retiring PC plod put into plain—very plain—clothes and ordered to follow her. Manpower shortage in the CID or something.

How could they suspect her? She was careful, *very* careful, especially since the radio van was gone. But that still could mean trouble. It meant trouble very near home. *I think that perhaps they are on to me*, she thought. *Kowalski has gone incommunicado. I just don't seem to get decent and loyal help*, her brain moaned, vilifying the unfortunate late Mr Kowalski and unconsciously echoing him. That operation was junked, after all her careful planning.

Fury welled up in her and she swore, loud and long and unladylike, in English, Polish, and Bulgarian. Her world was again crumbling. But if she went down, she wouldn't go alone!

Determinedly, she put on her coat, collected a stack of pennies, reminded herself of an emergency number, and, squaring her shoulders, went out. Maybe it was time to mention recruiting Vanessa. Maybe a new operation could arise from the ashes.

I will not give up! she snarled silently. *I will NOT give up! Every month, a strike for freedom and a new world order.* Then she could dump poor ineffective David and take her proper place.

And there he was: that pig clown. *Well, we will see!* Sandra stalked determinedly down the road.

14

I T WAS ABOUT 10.30. I HAD FOLLOWED SMITHY FOLLOWING SANDRA Stephens when she walked the dogs. When she returned, I got on to Smithy's walkie-talkie.

"I reckon she's convinced," he said. "I reckon she made me straight off, but I took time to let her check me out. Now she's hooked and spooked. Get Karen, Alan, and Ken over here, Bill. Pronto. She's very jittery."

They were in there in about two and a half seconds. And we didn't have long to wait. A very jerky-looking Sandra Stephens left hurriedly, just as a very confused David Stephens drove his BMW in from his Masonic dinner. A brief altercation, and Sandra sailed off, a man-o'-war under full canvas, leaving David standing there, open-mouthed. Smithy came on his walkie-talkie again.

"Bill, grab him. Karen, Alan, Ken, follow me"

"Got you, Smithy, on our way!"

As the strange procession trailed off into the night, I walked purposefully over to David Stephens. "Excuse me, sir," I said, flashing the warrant card. "Have you just been driving that car?"

"Yes, officer, why?"

"Would you let me see your license, sir?"

"Why, officer? What's the matter?"

"Well, sir, perhaps I shouldn't be saying this ..." I was at my most portentous and Plod-like "... but I know you're well thought of down at the nick. A BMW just like yours has been involved in a hit-and-run, and we are on the lookout for the car involved." I continued my suspicious pacing round the car until I noticed a fortuitous small dent in the front wing.

"Aha!" I said. "Where has this come from, sir?"

"I ... er, I don't know, officer. I can't explain it."

"Would you come down to the station for forensic checks? It shouldn't take long."

Poor old D. Stephens was more or less hustled into the car and made to run me down to the police station, where he was tested with a newfangled breathalyser (he was just on the limit) and ensconced in a waiting room with a non-threatening cup of coffee and a dolly-bird WPC.

Meanwhile, I conducted a three-way conversation with the station superintendent and a disembodied Whitehall mandarin-voice on the phone for authorisation to keep David Stephens on ice whilst his missus did the business. This was a protracted process and more trouble than arresting six sociopathic boa constrictors, but I eventually emerged—mangled, irritated, and sweaty—with a promise to keep David Stephens out of the way for a few hours. Poor guy, he was the one I felt sorry for. He'd had a bum steer all down the line.

Meanwhile, Sandra had led Smithy and Karen all around Presborough. When it seemed credible, Smithy had allowed her to dump him. In the bus station was a double-exit ladies' loo, so Smithy loitered at the wrong door as Ken and Alan continued to leapfrog after her. Black faces were not unknown round Presborough, but I didn't want her making Karen, even though I wouldn't expect a middle-class arrogant parish-pump aristo to remember a mere servant girl. Neither were tough-looking faces in denim jackets unknown in that town.

Contented that she had shed her tail, Sandra made a beeline for the nearest phone and spent some twenty minutes making phone calls. She came out looking pleased. Then she went straight home. If she noticed that her husband's car was not in the drive, she didn't seem too bothered. She just went to bed.

Soon, the bug in the bedroom began to snore, so I went back to the station and sprung friend Stephens, who also went home. He too started snoring.

I rang up to rehire Grey's men to take over surveillance and went back to the motel. Once more, morality won out, and instead of being entertained by bumps and squeaks from Karen's room, I was edified from my Nessie-warmed bed by the thought of a celibate and frustrated Smithy.

Next morning, Smithy and I joined Ken, Alan, Nessie, and Karen for a jog. They had even got me to join them, though what the jacks and villains I normally associated with would think of me, I didn't like to imagine. I magnificently ignored female comparisons to a grampus.

Then we waited. Grey's pseudo-telephone-engineers had the job well in hand, and we didn't want the slightest chance of any of us being made by a very spooked and shaky Sandra Stephens.

At eleven, Smithy and Karen went on a walk. At twelve, they came back. At one, the phone rang. It was Grey's man. Five rough-looking characters and one smoothie had arrived at Sandra's house, and there seemed to be some sort of altercation in some sort of wog language, he reported.

"OK, lads, this is it!" said Smithy, bright-eyed and bushy-tailed. "Ken, you and Bill cover the back door. Alan, you and me take the front. And then we ..."

"Ahem," came a very dignified and long-suffering cough from behind. "What about me?"

"Oh no," Smithy said. "No chance, no way, no how."

"So what's the matter, Massa? Ain't us poh black folks good enough for y'all? Ah's only a mere wummun."

"Stupid woman," said Smithy fondly.

"Well then, you great long string bean, I refuse categorically to be left out. After all, look what happened last time you left me behind! Black eye and fat lip! And it's not as though I'm the shrinking violet type. I've put Bill here on his back as well!"

Now why did she have to bring that up?

Then Nessie chipped in, "I'll drive, then you lot can just pile out."

Eventually, Smithy capitulated. Karen could come. Nessie could drive us. Karen and Nessie could wait in the car. Of course, I believed totally that they would stay in the car when I caught the sight of pigs winging overhead.

I further doubted Karen's motives when I saw her slip a length of iron pipe down her jeans.

On the way, Ken asked, "Isn't it a bit dangerous, seven of them and four of us?"

The righteous silence from the girls was deafening.

"Well, if you like, we'll wait until they get reinforcements and make it a bit fairer," I said. Smithy just smiled abstractedly. I knew what he'd be doing. He'd be praying. Asking that God of his not to think him too naughty if he splashed a villain or two.

With a gentle slowing motion, Nessie ghosted the 1100 to park behind the telecom van. No *Hawaii Five-0* tyre screeches here. She's got brains, this lass of mine.

An overalled Grey's man moved casually to meet us. But his words were far more urgent.

"Glad you lot are here. Don't know what they're saying, but it's getting heated in there!"

Smithy got out of the 1100, stretched, and strolled over to the telecom van. He emerged with five yellow helmets and five donkey jackets for local colour, and we all put them on and deployed round the van.

The tape recorder was making a great play of recording the gibberish that Smithy said was Bulgarian. It was all Sandra and Smoothie. The other five didn't seem to have the brains to understand English, let alone Bulgarian.

Eventually, some sort of compromise was met, because Sandra turned to speaking English and, in the clear, high, patronising tone that the English middle classes, however scrubberly, save for their inferiors and foreigners, Sandra began to instruct them about dissolving quietly into the background.

An argument broke out. The five local villains, all sounding just like they were in Z-cars—except theirs wasn't an act—were demanding money, and lots of it.

We were in a quandary. We'd stayed so low-key we hadn't applied for a warrant. We needed an excuse to go in warrantless. After about five minutes, we got it. Good old Sandra. The argument about money wound up tighter and tighter and noisier and noisier. She apparently didn't approve of the hooligans' demands.

"But that's robbery," she said.

"OK, lads, we all heard that! Go!" Smithy bellowed.

We shot out of the van, Ken and I armed with S&Ws, running to the back door while Smithy and Alan armed with a sledgehammer ran to the front. Smithy also had his faithful nunchaku.

One swing of the sledge demoralised the deadlock, and Smithy ran in, yelling, "Police, freeze!"

Perhaps the villains were TV critics, because the answer was a burst from a sawn-off shotgun. Smithy dived one way and Alan the other, and the shot pattered harmlessly onto the drive. But straight after came the *brrrp!* of a Sten. Those villains might be thick, but they were quick!

At the same time, the back door burst open, and villains came boiling out. Ken and I had a brisk few minutes incapacitating them, but eventually, at the expense of a bent nose and a face-full of dandruff for me and a sliced finger for Ken, we had four villains unconscious and handcuffed.

As we ran through the back door, the machine-gun's flatulence culminated in a great roaring explosion, and we were greeted by a blood-spattered headless smoothie with a banana-skin machine-gun in its hands. There's only so much a 25-year-old gun can take.

The toughie with the sawn-off shotgun surrendered in silence, horrified by the body and the blood-and-flesh splattered silence, and the smoke cleared to reveal a miraculously undamaged Alan and Smithy. Whilst we were picking them up, Sandra appeared from somewhere with a tiny .22 pistol and shot the stairs, the wall, and the hall mirror, but thankfully not us. As we dived for cover, she ran screaming out of the front door—straight for Smithy.

But Karen, lurking in the background, Masai warrior blood thoroughly up at the two threats to her man, streaked across the drive, grabbed Sandra by the hair and one lapel, hurled her six feet into the air, and applied *okuri-eri-jime*—a sliding-collar strangle.

"Will one of yez come and gerrer before I kill 'er," she screamed in purest Scouse.

Sandra was quickly handcuffed and the toy .22 collected for evidence, whilst Smithy and Karen collapsed on each other in an orgy of pride and anxiety.

We had an hour or two's anticlimax whilst five villains were fingerprinted, docketed, and banged up and a blood-wagon was sent for Smoothie. And then we all collapsed in a relieved heap at the motel. It's amazing—we should have been leaping all over the place at the successful conclusion of a case, but all we felt was depression. We thought of Ted; of all the dead innocent mugs who had just been passing by; of a Bulgarian embassy that encouraged its denizens to go freelance just for nuisance value, and which would play the diplomatic immunity card and be allowed to disclaim all responsibility for a smooth terrorist.

Reaction: it'd wear off.

Smithy and I cobbled together a suitable sanitised final report to my Beloved Führers in the Home Office, copies to Officer I/C Mugglesby, Grey's, and all the police forces who had helped us, with much gratitude, and making sure no stain was on my and Smithy's characters. There was no mention of a blonde bombshell buyer, and not much about a black special constable. We thanked Ken and Alan in person in the posh restaurant non-top of the Post Office tower in Liverpool.

And so we all lived happily ever after—apart from Ted, Kowalski, the Bulgarian, and a few hundred innocent bystanders down the years, of course. The injured Liverpool copper was given consultant status and went on to train police dogs and handlers.

We eventually got intelligence that a hard-line Bulgarian faction within the embassy had somehow got wind of lunatic little bubbles in the rehabilitation camps and a mad dog in the usually well-balanced Polish community—and, always on the lookout for trouble to make, had set them loose to cause as much random mayhem as possible.

When we interrogated Sandra, much more came to light. We would have liked a cross-reference, because Sandra's mind was going rapidly. After all, twenty-six years of general paralysis of the insane brought on by syphilis, culminating in the shock of being hurled yards in the air just when you think you've broken free, isn't really good for one's mental stability. We didn't get our cross-reference. The Bulgarian smoothie was dead and the five English thickies were only hired roughnecks, so we made do with Sandra.

It seemed that the idea of using old radios for communications was Sandra's. She was paranoid about phone taps and, being an ex-WAAF signaller, knew that radio five-letter groups were virtually unbreakable. But virtually isn't absolutely.

Eventually, we got the picture together. The Bulgarians' contribution to the March of World Communism was a low-cost, ramshackle little outfit beavering away at destabilisation and earning points with Papa Bear. Low-cost, ramshackle, and made up of British hired thugs, a lunatic and has-been woman, and a mad-bull Pole, it still caused us a lot of trouble. And caused a lot of people to get dead before their time.

Sandra now sits quite happy in Moss Side Top Security Hospital, where she picks the daisies off the wallpaper. Her husband, David, still drives down there once a fortnight. He thought her radio gear was a ham network. He seems better off without her; it can't be easy living with a schizophrenic syphilitic.

Smithy and Karen got married the other week. Rev. D. Atkinson officiated. I attended; weddings bore me and there wasn't even a bar, but Nessie enjoyed it. Karen looked gorgeous. If she wasn't a Bible-basher and hadn't hurled me over her shoulder, I could fancy her myself. Smithy looked like the most self-satisfied stork you've ever seen.

They scraped together enough money to buy a modest house in Formby, the posh coastal suburb of Liverpool. He works at home— freelance Russian translation—and Karen is completing her degree before going into teaching. There's some talk of Smithy training for church ministry They settled down in connubial bliss, going jogging along the sand, going to church twice on Sunday. For them, it was the life of Riley. I went back to villains and clubs and no-strings-attached Nessie.

It seemed good to all of us. And so we lived happily ever after ... for a while.

Printed and bound by CPI Group (UK) Ltd, Croydon, CR0 4YY